• A NERO WOLFE MYSTERY •

SILVER SPIRE

Robert Goldsborough

BANTAM BOOKS

NEW YORK • TORONTO • LONDON • SYDNEY • AUCKLAND

This edition contains the complete text
of the original hardcover edition.
NOT ONE WORD HAS BEEN OMITTED.

SILVER SPIRE

A Bantam Book / November 1992
Bantam paperback edition / January 1994

ISBN 0-553-56387-4

Published simultaneously in the United States and Canada

Bantam Books are published by Bantam Books, a division of Bantam
Doubleday Dell Publishing Group, Inc. Its trademark, consisting of the words
"Bantam Books" and the portrayal of a rooster, is Registered in U. S. Patent
and Trademark Office and in other countries. Marca Registrada. Bantam
Books, 1540 Broadway, New York, New York 10036.

PRINTED IN THE UNITED STATES OF AMERICA

RAD   0 9 8 7 6 5 4 3 2 1

To Barbara Stout

and

Rebecca Stout Bradbury

for their continuing
encouragement and
enthusiasm

SILVER SPIRE

ONE

With two baritone belches of the horn, the *Samuel I. Newhouse* eased from its slip at South Ferry, and we were on the briny. It being the middle of the day, only a couple of dozen people or so were scattered throughout the big boat, most of them either reading or dozing or trying to wriggle into comfortable positions on the molded, one-size-fits-all blue plastic seats.

The interior of the ferry had all the charm of a warehouse, and after five minutes of trying to get comfortable myself, I went out onto the small deck at the bow and let the May breeze blow across my face. The Statue of Liberty and Ellis Island, New York's newest tourist attraction, were off to the right—make that the starboard, mate—and the Verrazano-Narrows Bridge arched gracefully to port, while dead ahead through the haze of New York Harbor, the low green hills of Staten Island began to take form.

That morning as I sat in the kitchen of Nero Wolfe's brownstone on West Thirty-fifth Street devouring wheatcakes and the *Times,* I recalled the last time I had been on Staten Island, which most New Yorkers don't even think of as part of the city—when they think of it at all. That was almost ten years ago, when Wolfe took a case involving an arrogant old art collector on the island whose prized Cézanne had been filched from his house and replaced with a good but not great copy.

All arrows pointed to the collector's crotchety and somewhat larcenous maid, but it turned out the switch had been pulled by a guy posing as a gas company employee who said he'd been sent out to find a leak in the line. Anyway, thanks to Wolfe's brainpower and my leg power, the phony gas man, a onetime art history student with a police record as long as a pickpocket's fingers, got nailed, the Cézanne was recovered, and our bank balance received a healthy and much-needed transfusion.

This time, however, I was venturing forth to the borough of Richmond on what both Wolfe and I considered far more momentous business. But then, I'm getting ahead of myself, so I'll start where they say you're supposed to start—at the beginning.

The beginning was a rainy May morning—a Thursday, for those among you who want specifics. Wolfe was upstairs in the brownstone's rooftop greenhouse puttering with his beloved orchids, as is his sacred routine from nine to eleven every morning and four to six in the P.M. I sat at my desk in the office, entering orchid-germination records into the personal computer, as is part of my own more or less sacred routine.

The doorbell rang at ten-seventeen, and because the brownstone's Most Valuable Player, chef Fritz Brenner, was out buying provisions that later would be part of three-star meals, I did the honors, walking down the hall and peering through the one-way glass in the front door. The visitor on the stoop was high-shouldered and barrel-chested, and in his vested charcoal pinstripe, he looked like a banker faced with the prospect of having to give a loan, or maybe he was just suffering gas pains. But he didn't seem like the type to carry a concealed weapon, so I swung the door open.

"Good morning," I said with gusto. "We already have a set of *Britannica*s and currently subscribe to no fewer than eleven magazines—I can show you the list. Also, everyone who lives here is well insured, and we are not in the market for a vacuum cleaner, a set of genuine horsehair brushes, or a food processor. Now, what can I do for you, or you for me?"

I didn't even get a lip twitch for my efforts. "I am here to seek Nero Wolfe's counsel," the banker-type intoned somberly. "May I assume that you are Archie Goodwin, his associate?"

"Assume to your heart's content," I said. "Before this conversation goes a single sentence further, however, I must warn you that Mr. Wolfe sees no one—repeat, no one—without an appointment. And because I am the keeper of the appointment book, I am keenly aware that you don't have one—an appointment, that is."

"Correct. I realize that I took a chance by coming here without telephoning first. Maybe that was an ill-conceived strategy, but I thought perhaps you, Mr.

Goodwin, would be willing to hear my supplication and decide whether it merits Mr. Wolfe's consideration."

"That's a lot of syllables, but I'm used to all that and more from my employer. Tell you what: If you promise not to toss too many more big words around, I'll hear your—what was it—supplication? No guarantees, though."

"No guarantees," the banker-type agreed, still poker-faced.

"Another thing," I told him, planting myself in the doorway. "Is it fair to assume that your parents gave you a name?"

"What? Oh, yes, of *course*." He made a pathetic stab at smiling. It was gas pains, I decided. "Please excuse my manners. My name is Lloyd Morgan, and I work very closely with the Reverend Barnabas Bay."

"Bay as in that big church I've read about over on Staten Island, the one with the bells-and-whistles TV show?"

"The Tabernacle of the Silver Spire." Morgan rolled the syllables around proudly, as if they themselves were holy. "We feel our televised service is quite tasteful, however."

"Well, anyway, that's the place," I said, ushering Morgan into the brownstone and down the hall to the office. I pointed him at the red leather chair in front of Wolfe's desk and slid in behind my own desk, swiveling to face him. "Mr. Wolfe is up playing with his orchids," I told our visitor, "and he won't be back down until eleven. But you have my undivided attention; what's the problem?"

Morgan considered the well-tended nails on his

thick fingers, then took what I assume was a thoughtful breath before making eye contact. "First off, Barney—that's what Father Bay asks everybody on the staff to call him—knows I'm here, although he doesn't entirely approve. He considers me a worrywart. That is the exact word he used: 'worrywart,' " Morgan said in an offended tone. "However, worrywart or not, I insisted that we needed outside help and informed him of Nero Wolfe, whom he'd never heard of."

"The poor fellow must be living in a state of sensory deprivation," I deadpanned. "Everyone has heard of Nero Wolfe, probably even those Sherpa guides up on Mount Everest." Okay, so I was having a little fun at the poor guy's expense, mainly because I knew he wouldn't pick up on it. He didn't. In fact, the expression on his round, slightly ruddy face remained unchanged, which is to say basically blank. No smile, no frown, no scowl, no nothing.

"Barney maintains an incredible schedule," Morgan went on without apology, defending his boss, which is always worth a few points in my book. "It seems like he's on the move every minute—a speech to the ministerial council in Newark, a benefit dinner for one of our shelters for the homeless in the Bronx, the mayor's prayer breakfast downtown. He probably doesn't always peruse the newspapers as thoroughly as he should."

"Maybe none of us does." I almost liked Morgan—but not quite. "Now that we've agreed on something, how do you see Nero Wolfe helping you and the good reverend?"

Morgan, who had primly declined my offer of coffee, did loosen to the extent of unbuttoning his suitcoat, which was progress. Then he cleared his throat several times, which was not. "Mr. Goodwin, may I assume that this conversation is utterly confidential?"

"You may, unless a crime has been committed, in which case, as a private investigator licensed by the sovereign state of New York, I am required to report said crime. No choice." Okay, so there have been a few times—make it quite a few—when I've done some fudging with that particular requirement.

Morgan tilted his head back, apparently trying to look superior. "No *actual* crime has been committed—yet. But we, at least some of us, are greatly concerned that one will be."

"So I gather. Go on."

More throat clearing. "You have, of course, never been to the tabernacle."

"Correct." I nodded with a smile, mildly irked by the "of course" but amused by the disapproval in his voice.

"Well," he sniffed, "then you probably aren't aware that we get a total of some twelve thousand every Sunday attending our three morning services plus our evening service."

"Impressive. But I gather one of those twelve thousand is causing you and your leader grief."

"What makes you think that?"

I shrugged. "Give me a shred of credit. Look, for the last few minutes, we've been tiptoeing around each other like two cautious welterweights in Round One. I could probably sit here for another hour or more trying to guess your problem, but I won't—I've got other things that I'm paid to do. Now, I suggest you unload whatever it is you've got and let me see it before I get on with the rest of my life."

"All right, it's just that this is difficult to talk about," Morgan said stiffly. "For the last six Sundays, we've gotten very disturbing notes in the offering pouch—all directed at Barney."

"Pardon my ignorance, but what's an offering pouch?"

Another superiority sniff. "As I am sure you know, most churches send plates down the pews for the offering—the collection, if you will. But some, and we are among them, circulate cloth or leather pouches through the congregation—they have handles and they're about this deep," he said, holding one palm about a foot above the other. "For one thing, it's easier to be private about your offering if you're giving cash, and for another, our sanctuary is so big that if we passed conventional plates, they'd all overflow—even if we had twenty of them. The pouches hold a great deal more than a plate."

"Okay, so what do these 'disturbing notes' say?"

Morgan looked to be having more gas pains. "I've brought them." He sighed, reaching into his suitcoat and drawing out a packet of folded sheets that were paper-clipped together. He eyed me for several seconds, trying to decide whether I was trustworthy. Apparently I passed his trust test, if only barely. He handed over the small bundle, but turned loose of it like a widow giving her Social Security check to a mugger.

"As I said, there are six notes," he told me. "They are arranged in the order in which they came."

I slipped the paper clip off, holding the sheets

by the edges so as not to add my fingerprints to heaven knows how many others already there. The white sheets all were the same size, six by nine inches, probably from the same pad, and each had a message hand-printed in capitals in black ink from a felt-tipped pen. Here they are, in sequence:

REV BAY: MISFORTUNE PURSUES THE SINNER. (PROVERBS 13:21)

REV. BAY: TAKE YOUR EVIL DEEDS OUT OF MY SIGHT (ISAIAH 1:16)

REVEREND BAY: THE STING OF DEATH IS SIN (I CORINTHIANS 15:56)

REV. BAY: DEATH IS THE DESTINY OF EVERY MAN (ECCLESIASTES 7:2)

REVER. BAY: YOU DESERVE TO DIE. (I KINGS 2:26)

REV. BAY: THE TIME IS NEAR (REVELATION 1:13)

"Pretty ominous-sounding stuff," I said to Morgan. "Does your Mr. Bay get this sort of message often?"

"Reverend Bay does *not*," he replied, squaring his shoulders and looking offended. "Oh, once in a while, we find a note in the offering pouch expressing disapproval—usually mildly—about something in a sermon or in some other part of the service, which isn't unusual in a church our size. But this . . ."

"What does Bay think about the notes?"

"He professes indifference," Morgan said irritably. "Feels it's just the doings of some 'misguided soul,' to use his words."

"You don't agree, of course, or you wouldn't be here."

"Mr. Goodwin, these are the work of a psychopath, someone who I believe is truly dangerous."

"Maybe that's the case," I conceded, flipping open my notebook. "You say these have been coming for six weeks, which figures—there are six of them. Along about the third Sunday, didn't you, or someone else at the church, get suspicious and start watching more closely as the collection was taken?"

Morgan flushed. "We should have, of course. But we—Barney, me, the rest of the staff—all believed this was the handiwork of a demented individual, perhaps someone who was just passing through New York and soon would be gone. We get a lot of one- or two-time visitors from out of town."

"Does Bay have any enemies? Or any secrets that would make him vulnerable to, say, blackmail?"

Lloyd Morgan shook his head almost violently. "No, sir, and I must tell you I resent that suggestion."

"Hold it right there. You walked in here—without an appointment, I hasten to point out—looking for help. Nobody twisted your arm to come. If you feel like doing any resenting, you can damn well do it outside, on your way back to Staten Island."

That deflated the boy's radials. He bit his lower lip and took an economy-sized breath. "I'm sorry. This has been stressful for all of us, and I guess it shows. As far as enemies, Barney doesn't have any that I'm aware of—or that he's aware of, to hear him talk. Oh, there are ministries in the New York area that are jealous of his success, but it's inconceivable that one of their members would resort to this sort of despicable behavior."

"Uh-huh. How would you describe the makeup of your flock?"

Morgan leaned back and laced his hands behind his head, which suggested that I was about to get more answer than I'd requested. "Mr. Goodwin, our membership, or 'flock,' as you so quaintly term it, is something over twelve thousand strong, and that's not to mention the hundreds of thousands in our 'electronic congregation,' who watch on TV from every single state, every Canadian province, and sixteen other countries, including Korea and the Philippines.

"Demographically, our members are a healthy mix. Of the twelve thousand plus, more than half are under thirty-five, and forty-four percent are single. And you'll probably be surprised to learn that almost four thousand of them live in Manhattan—many in the Village, East Village, and Soho. And several hundred ride over on the ferry weekly. Would you have guessed that?"

"Never," I said solemnly.

That brought forth a thin smile, which Wolfe would have described as smug. "I thought not," he said in a satisfied tone that made me yearn to help him out the door.

"Have you begun any type of internal investigation, or tried to at least figure out where the note-writer sits every week?"

"No. As I said before, we kept hoping it would . . . go away by itself."

"These things rarely do. What about the police?"

Morgan shuddered, and I noticed beads of perspiration on his ample forehead. "With due respect to the authorities, this is the last course we want to pursue—at least at this point. As you of course know, the past few years have been difficult ones for high-profile ministries, particularly ones with a television arm. Now, I don't for one instant mean to compare us with some of the evangelists you've heard all too much about in the media. But the fact is, because of them and the awful image they have, we are very skittish about any kind of publicity that could be construed as sensational. And we are naturally quite concerned that if we called in the authorities, word would inevitably get to the press. Now do you see why I asked earlier if our talk was confidential?"

"I do. But if the situation worries you as much as you indicate, doesn't it really warrant bringing in the police?"

"Perhaps eventually." Morgan nodded. "But we—Barney, me, the other church leaders—thought that we'd try an alternative first."

"All right. But there are a couple things you should know from the start. First, Mr. Wolfe doesn't come cheap, and—"

"We are prepared to meet all but the most exorbitant demands." You had to give the man credit; he raised pomposity to an art form.

"And you may well find Mr. Wolfe's demands exorbitant," I told him. "But second, and this you can't do a damn thing about, he also is far from the world's biggest fan of organized religion—regardless of who's doing the organizing. Now that I've said that, don't ever make the mistake of trying to duel with him over biblical quotes; he knows that book better than I know the batting averages of the last Mets championship team. And believe me, I can give you those figures right down to earned run averages."

Morgan passed a handkerchief across his dewy forehead and sighed. "So are you suggesting that we look elsewhere for aid?"

"Not necessarily. But I do feel you should know exactly how the cards lie, and frankly, I'm not sure you have openers. However, Mr. Wolfe will be in the office in twelve minutes, and I'll discuss the matter with him then. How can I reach you?"

Morgan reached into the breast pocket of his suit-coat and, after some fumbling, produced a calling card, a tasteful buff-colored number with his name in the center, the church's in the lower left corner, and the phone number lower right.

"Just for the record," I asked, "what's your role at the tabernacle?"

"Business manager," he sniffed. "A 'Mr. Inside,' if you will, while Barney of course is 'Mr. Outside.' He's our star, as it should be. He preaches almost every Sunday, and he's the one the TV audience sees. I'm just a paper-pusher back in the office." He smiled modestly—or maybe he wanted it to appear modest.

"One more thing," I told him. "I'd like to keep these notes, just long enough to show them to Mr. Wolfe. They may help pique his interest. I promise I'll return them to you intact—whether or not Mr. Wolfe takes the case."

Morgan looked at the notes doubtfully, then shrugged. "I didn't really intend to leave them.

Well . . . all right, if you promise that I'll get them back."

"I promise. Do you want a receipt?"

"No, no, your word is more than good enough, Mr. Goodwin," he said, not sounding as if he meant it.

"Okay, then this is all I need for now," I told him as I stood up.

He also got to his feet, looking uncertain. "When will I hear from you?"

"Today. Will you be in your office?"

He took thirty words to say he would, and I hustled him out as politely as possible, all the while reassuring him I would call him before day's end. I didn't like the odds of Wolfe accepting a commission from Morgan and Bay as clients. After all, as I had pointed out none too subtly to Morgan, Wolfe was about as likely to work for a church as he was to send Fritz out for a Quarter-Pounder for dinner. But I did have one bargaining chip with the Big Guy: The almighty bank balance was in serious need of nourishment.

TWO

Back at my desk after letting Morgan out, I still had five minutes before Wolfe's arrival from his morning séance with the blossoms. I put the time to use by calling Lon Cohen at the *New York Gazette*.

Lon has no title at the paper that I've ever heard of or seen in print, and his name is not on the paper's masthead. But he occupies an office next door to the publisher's on the twentieth floor, and he seems to know more about what goes on in New York, both aboveboard and below, than the city council and the police department combined. He has provided useful information to us on at least a gross of occasions, and we've reciprocated by giving the *Gazette* at least as many scoops. And, not incidentally, he also plays a mean hand of stud poker, as I rediscover to my sorrow almost every Thursday night at Saul Panzer's apartment, where several of us have gathered with the pasteboards for years.

"Morning," I said after he'd answered his phone

with the usual bark of his name. "Got a minute for a friend?"

"I haven't got a minute for my mother, let alone the mother of my children. What makes you special?"

"Ah, a bit on the testy side today, are we? You shouldn't be terse with someone who so thoughtfully lined your pockets with lettuce at the gaming table a week ago this very day."

"I *did* have a pretty fair night, didn't I?" Lon responded, sounding almost mellow. "All right, what do you need to know? And what's in it for me?"

"Now there's a cynical attitude," I said. "See if I raise tonight when you've got a pair showing."

"Archie, I'd just love to go on bantering all morning, but at the risk of sounding like somebody from *The Front Page,* we've got a paper to put out."

"And a fine paper it is, me lad. Okay, what can you tell me in a few well-chosen sentences about the Reverend Barnabas Bay and his church over on Staten Island?"

"Bay? He's got a reputation for being smart, damned smart. Comes originally from someplace down south, maybe Georgia. He's built a big following here in just a few years, and a huge building. Its name is a little too show bizzy for me—the Tabernacle of the Silver Spire. It's got that name because the church, which is nondenominational, is topped by a metal spire, stainless steel or aluminum, I suppose, that dwarfs everything else around it. Controversial when it was built. But, at least according to our religion writer, Bay's several cuts above the televangelists who've supplied us with so many juicy headlines in the none-too-distant past. By all accounts, he's honest, earnest, and one hell of a spellbinder in the pulpit."

"Any hint of scandal?"

"Not that's come my way. No personal stuff I've ever heard about. He's got a wife who's a knockout, and I think four kids. About two years back, a handful of churches on the island and over in Jersey complained that they'd lost parishioners to him, but that happens all the time. Might just be that he's giving 'em something they weren't getting from their local pastors."

"The guy sounds too good to be true."

"That's exactly what I told Walston—he's our religion writer—after reading the Sunday piece he did on Bay a while back. But Walston swears that's the real Bay. And the padre puts his money—or the church's money—where his mouth is. The Silver Spire has set up several shelters for battered women and the homeless in Manhattan, and the church supplies all the money and staffing to support them, the works. Okay, I've given you more than a few sentences; what can you give me, as in, one: Why is Wolfe interested in Bay? And, two: Does the good reverend have feet of clay after all?"

"I don't have answers, because I don't know myself—honest. But you can rest assured that if anything happens, you'll be hearing from us."

"Yeah, and the check's in the mail, right?" Lon growled, signing off with a mumble that sounded remotely like "good-bye." After cradling the receiver, I just got the day's mail opened and stacked on Wolfe's blotter before the groaning of the elevator heralded his arrival from on high.

"Good morning, Archie, did you sleep well?" he

asked as he detoured around the desk and settled into the chair constructed specifically to support his seventh of a ton. It's a question he's asked on thousands of mornings.

"Like a baby," I answered, as I have on thousands of mornings.

So much for one of our daily rituals. He spun through the mail quickly, saw that it held nothing of interest, then pushed the buzzer on the underside of his desk. It squawks in the kitchen, signaling Fritz to bring beer—specifically, two bottles of Remmers. He then picked up his current book, *Mars Beckons*, by John Noble Wilford, which he was intending to read until lunch.

"Before you get smitten with the idea of hitching a ride on the next Mars-bound rocket, we had a visitor this morning," I told him.

He set the book down deliberately and looked peevish. It's his normal expression when his routine is messed with. I got an "All right, what is it?" glare, although his lips didn't move.

"A gentleman stopped by," I began as Fritz entered silently, bearing a tray with two bottles of beer and a pilsner glass. "This gentleman's boss is getting threatening notes, and he wants to hire you to find out who's penning them."

The peevish expression remained as Wolfe poured beer and watched the foam settle. "Continue," he said coldly.

"You know as well as I do what the current state of our finances is," I responded.

Wolfe drew in air and let it out slowly, keeping his narrowed eyes on me. "Archie, you are maundering," he snorted. "I am painfully aware that I will get no peace until you have unburdened yourself. Let's get on with it."

This was going to be tricky. "You remember how you once said that a client's line of work is far less important than the problem he presents to us?"

"I expressed that thought in relation to a specific and unusual situation, as you well remember."

"Through the years, we've had a lot of unusual situations, and for my money, we have another one." I looked at Wolfe and got no encouragement, but I've never been one to let that stop me. "The man on the receiving end of the threatening notes is well-known," I went on. "Maybe you've heard of him; his name is Barnabas Bay."

"Pah. A clerical mountebank."

"Pah yourself. I know you have a lot of respect for the knowledge and opinions of our friend Mr. Cohen. He tells me that Bay is far from a mountebank, and that—"

"You don't even know the definition of the word," Wolfe challenged.

"Wrong. I looked it up after it had been used to describe *you* by someone in this very room a few years back. And at that, she was the second person to call you a mountebank. One more and I'm going to start believing it. Anyway, Lon describes Bay as smart, honest, earnest, and a top-drawer preacher to boot. To say nothing of the good works his church does, among them shelters here in Manhattan for battered women and the homeless."

"Commendable," Wolfe answered without conviction. "Suggest that he talk to the police about the notes."

"I did, but, at least according to his sidekick, Lloyd Morgan—he's the man who stopped by—Bay is trying to avoid the kind of publicity that might result from an investigation."

"Given his line of work, his reaction would seem a prudent one," Wolfe said.

"That sounds suspiciously like a cheap shot," I told him. "How about asking me for a verbatim report of my chat with Mr. Morgan?"

Wolfe sighed and closed his eyes, probably hoping I would disappear. "It appears that I'll get one whether I want it or not. Go ahead."

In the past, I've recounted conversations of hours in length to Wolfe without omitting a single word, so this shorty was a snap. I ended by placing the hate notes found in the collection plates in front of him. "Here, you may find these interesting," I said.

Wolfe made a face but studied the sheets in silence for ninety seconds, careful not to touch them with his fingertips. "Anyone with a concordance could have done this all in ten minutes, fifteen at most," he said, waving a hand.

"Okay, I'm willing to concede that there's a gap in my knowledge: what's a concordance?"

"A refreshing admission. It is a biblical subject index. Many Bibles have them in the back. Return these to Mr. Morgan," he said curtly, pushing the notes in my direction.

"What should I tell him?"

"To go to the police, of course," he snapped, picking up his book. If I've learned anything at all about the foibles of genius in the years of living in the same household with one, it's knowing when to keep after him and when to back off. This was one of those times to back off—if only for a while. I left Wolfe to his beer and book and busied myself with the orchid-germination records, which kept me occupied until lunchtime.

Among the unwritten rules in the brownstone is that business—and that includes prospective business—is not to be discussed during meals. So as we feasted on Maryland crab cakes and Fritz's Caesar salad with garlic croutons, Wolfe held forth on the advisability of the United States reorganizing into about a dozen states—certainly no more than fifteen. I mostly listened, chewed, and nodded, although I did ask who the rest of the country would make jokes about if there wasn't a California to kick around anymore.

As usual, we returned to the office after lunch for coffee, but I still wasn't ready to renew the Bay campaign. Wolfe read until it was time to visit his orchids at four, while I balanced the checkbook, paid the bills, and reread the *Gazette*'s account of the zany Mets game against Cincinnati at Shea, in which our boys scored six runs in the second inning on only one hit, a bunt single. Shows you what can happen when the opponents make three errors, hit a batter, give you three walks, and throw a wild pitch.

After Wolfe went upstairs, I called Morgan, who picked up on the first ring. "You talked to him?" he blurted before I could spit out anything other than my name.

"Yes, but I have nothing definite to report. We're going to discuss your problem again later."

"Oh, dear, that doesn't sound terribly encouraging, does it?"

"Now, I didn't say that. I promised to report today, though, and I wanted to make sure I caught you before you went home. I'll phone you again in the morning."

Morgan didn't sound tickled with the news, but that was his problem; I had my own—getting Wolfe to take a church as a client. I tried him again when he came down from the plant rooms at six, and I'll spare you the grim details, other than to say that he got so angry with my badgering, as he calls it, that he stalked out of the office, retreating to his bedroom until dinnertime. And following dinner, as we got settled in the office with coffee, I tried once more, pointing out to Wolfe that he didn't have to go near the Silver Spire church himself.

"As usual, I'll do all the on-site work," I told him, "and for that matter, you don't have to be exposed to Bay or any of his religious types until the very end, when you've figured the thing out."

My answer was a glower and two sentences: "Archie, let me save your larynx further exercise on this subject. Under no circumstances will I accept a commission from Mr. Bay or his organization."

"Uh-huh. The bank balance be hanged, eh? What do you suggest I say to Morgan?"

Wolfe turned a hand over. "Tell him whatever you like. This is not the first time we have rejected an entreaty, nor is it likely to be the last."

"Keep your pronouns in the singular where

they belong," I shot back. "*I* didn't reject anything."

Wolfe glowered again and retreated behind his book, which gave me some satisfaction, but not much. I contemplated quitting, something I've done for varying periods at least a dozen times over the years, but vetoed the idea because my vacation was coming up in less than a month, and Lily Rowan and I had all our reservations for two weeks in England and Scotland. True, I had a respectable amount squirreled away in savings and a few investments, but I was damned if I was going to let Wolfe off the hook for my well-earned furlough—with pay.

Fortunately, I had a good reason to leave the brownstone that night, thereby possibly saving Wolfe from being brained with a blunt object and me from being booked on a murder charge. It was Thursday, meaning I had the above-mentioned engagement with cards and chips—both the poker and potato variety— at Saul's place over on Thirty-eighth just east of Lexington. And this time, I was the big winner, while Lon—who never once mentioned Barnabas Bay— went home with empty pockets.

The next morning, while Wolfe was up communing with the orchids, I called Lloyd Morgan from my desk in the office. "Sorry to be the bearer of bad news," I told him, "but Mr. Wolfe does not feel he can accept your problem."

I could hear an intake of air. "I was afraid of that," Morgan groaned. "I gather that decision is irreversible?"

"I'm afraid so."

Another deep breath. "Is there . . . anyone else

you could recommend? Perhaps another investigator?"

For those of you who are new to these precincts, when the need arises, as it frequently does, Wolfe employs two free-lances—Saul Panzer and Fred Durkin. Saul doesn't look like much: barely five-seven, skinny, stoop-shouldered, usually in need of a shave, and with a face that's two-thirds nose. But he's got a sharper pair of eyes than Willie Mays in his prime, and when assigned to follow someone, he sticks to him—or her—like epoxy. He's also in constant demand, and has more work than he can handle, although he'll almost always drop whatever he's doing for Wolfe.

Fred Durkin is another story. He's big—make that thick—somewhat on the slow side, and a long way from brilliant. Loyalty and honesty are two of his strong suits, though. And while he's no Saul, he's tenacious and damn good as a tail. Through the years, Wolfe has used him almost as much as Saul, but of late, business has been slow, which Fred has complained to me about more than once. Maybe this was one part of the reason I was leaning Fred's way when Morgan posed his question. The other part was that the job didn't seem all that complicated on the surface.

Maybe you'd have done it differently. If so, I wish you'd been around that Friday morning to stop me before I gave Fred's telephone number to Lloyd Morgan. Then you wouldn't be reading this.

THREE

For the next eleven days, I barely gave a thought to the Tabernacle of the Silver Spire or to Lloyd Morgan or Fred Durkin. Part of the reason was that I had nudged Wolfe into accepting an honest-to-goodness case—although not a very exciting one—involving a small supermarket chain whose largest store, up in Westchester County, was coming up short on its receipts almost every day. The culprit, as Wolfe suspected early on based on my nosing around the store for two days, was a debt-laden assistant manager who had two accomplices—a pair of rosy-cheeked checkout girls, both teenagers, with the most innocent faces this side of a convent. Our fee wasn't breathtaking, but given that the whole business took less than a week, we had no reason to complain.

Another distraction—a pleasant one—was that La Rowan got more fired up by the day about our trip to Merrie Olde, and that enthusiasm started to rub off on yours truly, to the point that I was digesting guidebooks about places like the Lake Country and the Cotswolds and Loch Lomond. Oh, I did hear from Fred once, the very day I'd recommended him to Morgan. He called to find out what I knew about the church, as well as to ask why Wolfe had shied away from accepting the case.

"Mr. Wolfe avoids most things having to do with formal religion," I told him. I also gave him my impressions of Morgan, along with Lon's comments about Bay as a preacher and spiritual leader. I signed off by saying, "Good luck, and give a holler if you need anything," and I sent the threatening notes back to Morgan in a sealed envelope—at my expense—via Herb Aronson, for my money the most dependable cabbie in New York.

The holler, when I got it, came from another quarter. It was a Tuesday morning about nine, and I was in the office typing up letters Wolfe had dictated the day before, when the phone rang.

"Okay, Archie, better catch me up, and fast!" It was Lon Cohen, and the exclamation mark I put on the end of his sentence doesn't do justice to the urgency in his voice.

"Catch you up on what?"

"You know damn well what," he blurted. "The Silver Spire business, and Durkin."

"What about Durkin?" Now I was almost shouting myself, and my throat suddenly got as dry as Death Valley.

"As if you didn't know. He's been tossed in the slammer—for murder."

"Wha-a-a-t? How did—"

"Dammit, Archie, stop jerking me around. We're coming up on deadline, and I've got to have something fast. The boss knows Durkin's practically an employee of Wolfe's, and he's all over me to come up with an exclusive on this."

My brain was racing to keep pace with my mouth. "Bay's *dead*?"

"Not *Bay*," Lon snapped irritably. "An assistant of his. Are you going to help me, or not?"

"Time out," I said. "First, Mr. Wolfe—through me—was approached by one of the Silver Spire staff because of a problem they were having; that's when I called you to find out about Bay. But Mr. Wolfe wasn't excited at the idea of having a church on his client list, so we recommended Fred."

Lon snorted. "I think I've been around you long enough to know you wouldn't throw Durkin to the dogs just to save your hide and Wolfe's. So you're giving it to me straight?"

"As straight as William Tell's arrow. Who got killed, and when?"

"Guy named Royal Meade, the senior associate pastor, and Bay's Number-Two person on the staff. Durkin shot him sometime last night in one of the church offices."

"Bull. Did Fred confess?"

"All right, *allegedly* shot him. Anyway, he's downtown in the lockup. I'm surprised you hadn't heard about it. Now, just what kind of problem was the church having?"

"That's going to have to wait until I've spoken to my employer."

"Come on, Archie. We need—"

"Look, I've got to talk to Wolfe, and then I'll get back to you—I promise. Has a bond been set?"

"Oh, sure, you want information, but you're not willing to cough any up yourself," he snapped. "As far as bond, I don't know."

I vowed to Lon that he'd hear from me before the morning was over, and I signed off, taking the stairs two at a time to the plant rooms. In the cool room, which is the first one you enter, I tried not to be dazzled by the reds and whites and yellows of the *Odontoglossums,* but as often as I've been up on the roof, I never get used to the breathtaking sight of those and the other show-offs that make up the ten thousand orchids Wolfe refers to as his "concubines." I passed on through the moderate and tropical rooms, steeling myself against the charms of the cattleyas and miltonias.

Wolfe, wearing a yellow smock, was in the potting room, planted on his stool at the bench. He was glumly considering a panicle of *Oncidium altissimum,* while Theodore Horstmann, Wolfe's full-time orchid nurse, was at the sink washing out pots.

Wolfe's expression didn't improve when he spotted me in the doorway. "Yes?" he grunted.

"We've got a problem, or you know damn well I wouldn't be up here," I said as old Horstmann threw a glare my way. He glares at me even when I'm not trespassing in his sanctuary, though. He doesn't like me, but that's okay, because the feeling is mutual and has been for years. I returned the glare, which sent him back to washing his pots.

"Durkin's in jail on a murder charge," I told Wolfe. "You recall I told you he took the Silver Spire job that you nixed. Well, some guy named Meade on the church staff got himself shot dead last night, and Lon called to tell me they've charged Fred."

"Preposterous."

"Agreed. What do we do?"

He drew in air and looked down at the panicle in his hand before gently placing it on the bench. "Confound it, get Mr. Parker—now."

Wolfe yields to no one in his distaste for the legal profession. However, he makes an exception for Nathaniel Parker, who has been his attorney for years and is one of the few men of any occupation he will shake hands with and invite to dinner. I went to the extension on the potting-room wall and punched out Parker's number from memory. "Nero Wolfe calling," I told his secretary, who put me through, and I handed the receiver to Wolfe.

"Mr. Parker, Nero Wolfe. Yes, I am well, thank you. One of my associates, Fred Durkin, whom you have met, has been charged with murder. . . . No, the circumstances are unclear. I'm putting Archie on to give you those few particulars he knows. . . . Yes, I am prepared to post bond." He handed the instrument to me, and I unloaded what Lon had given me. Parker took it in, said we'd be hearing from him shortly, and hung up. I cradled the phone, turning to Wolfe.

"Okay, you're rid of me for now—except that I promised Lon I'd give him something for the next edition. We owe him that much for his call. I'd like to at least tell him about the love notes."

His chin dipped almost imperceptibly, which for him constitutes a nod. He was so peeved at the interruption in his precious routine that he would have agreed to almost anything to get rid of me. As I walked out, I looked over my shoulder; Wolfe already had turned his attention back to the ailing *Oncidiums*, but Horstmann was at the sink eyeing me, probably afraid I'd walk off with something, like maybe an empty pot. I gave him a smile and a wink.

FOUR

By the time Wolfe came down from the plant
rooms, I had called Lon and read him the
text of the six notes to Bay, which earned me a hurried
thanks. And Parker had phoned as well. "He says he
can spring Fred," I told Wolfe as he settled behind his
desk and rang for beer. "It'll cost us fifty big ones."

"Get the money. What else did Mr. Parker learn?"

"Not much. It seems that—" I was interrupted
by the front doorbell, and since Fritz was out, I went
down the hall and took a look through the one-way
glass, making a fast return trip to the office. "It's old
you-know-who," I told Wolfe. "Instructions?"

A sigh. "Let him in," he said without enthusiasm
as the bell sounded again, this time one long, impatient squeal.

"Good morning, Inspector, nice to see you," I
said, throwing open the door and allowing admittance
to Lionel T. Cramer, head of Homicide for the New
York Police Department. He growled and barreled by
me like a freight train that had lost its brakes. I was

two strides behind him as he thundered into the office and plopped into the red leather chair, pulling a cigar from the breast pocket of his navy blue suitcoat and jamming it unlit into his mouth.

"Sir?" Wolfe murmured, raising his eyebrows and looking up from an orchid catalog that had just arrived in the mail.

"I'll 'sir' you," Cramer spat. "This house has meant nothing but trouble for me through the years. Way back when, there was that poor devil Johnny Keems. And then Cather. And God knows, I've aged because of you and this one," he rasped, pointing a finger more or less in my direction. "And now Durkin. I never thought he was the smartest guy in town, but I sure didn't have him pegged. Cather was no bargain—that never surprised me.* But Durkin does."

"Please, Mr. Cramer," Wolfe said, his voice still soft. "Archie and I only recently learned of the charge against Fred. We would appreciate any details."

"Hah! I'm sure you would. Durkin says he wasn't working for you, but I don't believe it any more than I believe that college basketball is an amateur sport."

"He is telling the truth," Wolfe said evenly.

"Uh-huh." Cramer gnawed on his stogie. "Then why did one of the people at that Silver Spire church say they'd started out by coming to see Goodwin?"

"That is also true. Archie, tell Mr. Cramer of the visit from Mr. Morgan—all of it."

I recited the whole thing, including Wolfe's steadfast refusal to accept the case, my referral of Fred to

---

*A *Family Affair,* by Rex Stout.

Morgan, and Fred's one call to me to learn more about the Silver Spire operation. "And that's all I knew about it until Lon Cohen phoned me this morning with the news that Fred had been charged," I said to the inspector.

He scowled at me, then at Wolfe and back at me. "Okay, maybe you're leveling, maybe not; with you two, I can't always tell. Here's what we know, and it's probably fairly accurate, because both Durkin and the Silver Spire people—and that includes their big kahuna, Barnabas Bay—tell it the same way, at least up to a point.

"First off, and you both obviously know this, Bay had been getting those nasty Bible verse notes slipped into the Sunday collection bags. The church could have come to us about it, but did they? No—because they were afraid of bad press. And now look what they've got themselves. Can you imagine the headlines this afternoon and tomorrow? And the TV news? Hah! Anyway, they hired Durkin to find out who was writing the damn things, and from what we've been told, he prowled around the church off and on for more than a week, including on two Sundays. He apparently alienated at least some of the staff, including Royal Meade, the guy who bought the farm last night, who had no use at all for him. From what I get, this Lloyd Morgan was the one pushing to hire a gumshoe. Nobody else was warm for the idea—they mostly felt the notes were the doing of a crank. But Morgan has Bay's ear, and he got the top man to go along with it."

"In what way did Fred alienate the church staff?" Wolfe asked.

Cramer leaned back and ran a hand over a ruddy cheek, frowning. "He told them he thought the notes were an inside job, that somebody on the payroll was writing them. Needless to say, that ticked everybody off, including even Morgan."

Wolfe drew in a bushel of air and exhaled slowly. "When did Fred drop this bomb?"

"Last night, at some sort of staff meeting. Apparently sent the place up for grabs. Anyway, sometime after the meeting broke up, Meade was found dead in his office, shot twice in the head with bullets from Durkin's thirty-eight. And Durkin's prints were the only ones on the weapon. He claims he'd hung his suitcoat on a hook in a hallway with the gun in its holster under it and—"

The doorbell rang, and with Fritz still out, I played butler. Cramer went on with his narrative as I walked to the front hall and peered through the one-way glass. Standing on the stoop was Nathaniel Parker, all six-feet-four of him, looking elegant and urbane in a three-piece brown suit and without a single salt-and-pepper hair out of place. And next to him, disheveled and drained, was Fred Durkin, who is about an inch shorter than my five-eleven but who hauls around at least fifteen pounds more than I do, maybe twenty. Droplets of perspiration covered the Irish forehead that continued unbroken to the top of his head, where a few tufts of red hair kept him from being classified as bald.

I opened the door, holding an index finger to my lips, and motioned them into the front room. "I'll be damned," I said once we all were in and I shut the door to the hall. "I've got questions, and so does Wolfe, but right now, Cramer's in with him, and you can guess what that conversation's about." Fred nodded numbly. "I'm going back. Sit tight until he's gone. And enjoy the magazines," I said, closing the door behind me.

As I reentered the office, Cramer was winding up his recap. ". . . anyway, your Durkin is dead meat, you can bank on it," he told Wolfe, making no attempt to keep the satisfaction out of his voice. "The only people who could've plugged Meade are Durkin and a bunch of sparkling-clean church honchos. Which leaves Durkin. Period."

Wolfe looked questioningly at me. "That was Mr. Wilson at the door," I told him. "He delivered your order."

He picked up on the verbal code and turned back to Cramer. "Your faith in the corporate character of religious leaders is heartwarming, although difficult to justify," Wolfe said. "I am sure you remember the priest last autumn who admitted helping himself to more than twenty thousand dollars from the collection plate over a period of years. And the deacon in that Protestant church on Long Island who beat a parishioner to death one night in the sanctuary when she resisted his advances. And the—"

"Oh, balls!" Cramer bellowed as he stood up. "You can sit there forever stewing in that smugness of yours, for all I care, but I'm telling you that you'd better find yourself another free-lance, because where Durkin's going, he's not going to be on call to do your keyhole-peeping chores anymore." He flung his cigar at the wastebasket, missing as usual, and left the office as fast as he'd entered. I trailed him down the hall to the front door, which he yanked open without my help, not bothering to close it behind him as he lumbered down the steps to the unmarked black sedan at the curb.

"All clear," I said, opening the door to the front room. Parker put down *The New Yorker* he'd been reading and unfolded himself, while Fred, who apparently had passed the time contemplating his shoe tips, struggled to his feet from the sofa, looking as if it took every bit of the energy he had. They followed me to the office, where Parker staked his claim to the red leather chair and Fred dropped into a yellow one.

Wolfe dipped his chin at them both, then looked at Parker, obviously awaiting an answer.

The lawyer shrugged. "I thought you'd be surprised to see us. Frankly, I'm a little surprised myself, at least by the speed of things. But the judge at the bond hearing is an old friend," he said, smiling sheepishly. "And he, well . . . owes me a favor or two, from way back. Our case for bail was strong anyway, even though it's a murder. Circumstantial evidence, no witnesses, a defendant with no previous record and not likely to flee the jurisdiction. Even though the media heat's going to be intense, the state—grudgingly—stipulated to the half-million figure, which I felt was reasonable, and which means of course that we put up ten percent." Fred, elbows on knees, continued looking at the floor.

"And the money?" Wolfe asked.

"Oh, I took care of that," Parker said with a casual wave of a hand. "I know you're good for it."

"Thank you, sir. Archie will supply you with a check today." He turned his attention to Fred, who even in tension-free situations is uncomfortable around Wolfe. Now he looked like a kid who'd been hauled into the principal's office after he'd been caught cheating on tests three times in a week.

"I would like a summary of your investigation, right up to the murder—no more than ten minutes," Wolfe said sharply, aware of Fred's tendency to ramble.

He ran a hand up his forehead. "Well, you know that Archie referred me for this job. I appreciate that, Arch, even with what's happened. Anyway, it was . . . uh, a week ago Saturday that I went over to Staten Island—that's some spread the church has there—and I met with Lloyd Morgan. He showed me the notes, six of 'em, which he said you both had already seen. He told me they wanted to find out who was writing them, and that I could have the run of the place, including evenings. I met a few of the staff, including Bay, that day."

"What was Mr. Bay's attitude toward you?" Wolfe asked.

Fred shrugged. "He seemed, I don't know, sort of embarrassed, like he wished the whole business would just go away. He didn't really seem to like the idea of having a P.I. around, although he was decent enough to me. Said he couldn't for the life of him think who'd write this sort of stuff to him."

"And you were there for Sunday services?"

"Two weeks running. I watched the collection being taken from different places in the balcony the first Sunday at all the services, and from the main floor the second Sunday. Nobody put nasty notes in either week, but if they had, you couldn't tell anyway.

They use these bags, and people put their hands right down into them with their money or whatever. It'd be easy to slip something small like a note in without anybody spotting it, even the person sitting next to you. I wanted to talk to the ushers who pass the offering bags, but Morgan said no; he didn't want a lot of people to know what was going on, for fear it would get out. Bad publicity."

Wolfe made a face. "As you know, Inspector Cramer was just here. He said you felt these missives were written by someone on the staff."

Fred nodded. "Yeah, and I probably shouldn't have said so until there was some way I could be more sure of it, but they—particularly Morgan—were pushing for a progress report. It sure caused a hell of a ruckus last night, and then—well . . ." He spread his hands.

"Of course, you were correct."

Fred looked at Wolfe with his mouth open. "You believe me?"

"Certainly. But tell us why you reached the conclusion the writer was on the church staff."

"Okay," he said with a hint of enthusiasm in his voice. "Morgan told me the only ones who knew that I was on the case were Bay's inner circle—eight people in all, and that includes Bay. Plus the dead man, Meade. The notes came for six straight Sundays, until the first Sunday that I showed up. Then they stopped."

"Possibly a coincidence," Wolfe remarked.

"Maybe," Fred said. "But there's this: After each service, the offering bags are taken to a walk-in vault in the basement by the ushers. The bags are put in the vault while one of that inner circle watches, and the vault is shut and locked after each service. The only people with the combination are those eight. The money—they get thousands in cash at every service, besides all the checks—doesn't get counted until Monday morning. In the meantime, any of the eight could have put a note in one of the bags."

"Speculation," Wolfe replied. "Any church member or visitor also could easily have slipped notes into a pouch undetected during the offering. You suggested that yourself."

"I thought you said you believed my theory," Fred responded with a hangdog expression.

"I do. Would anyone like something to drink? I'm having beer."

Parker and Fred opted for coffee, and Fred followed me out to the kitchen. Fritz was back, working on lunch, so I took on the responsibility for Wolfe's beer order, while Fred carried in two cups of coffee from the pot that is kept hot all morning. We got resettled in the office as Wolfe poured beer into his glass and dropped the bottle cap into his center desk drawer. Years ago, he got it in his head that he might be drinking too much beer, so he started keeping track by saving the bottle caps and counting them once a week. As far as I can tell, the bottle-cap census hasn't curbed his consumption one ounce.

"How many people at the church knew the purpose of your investigation?" he asked after taking a healthy swallow.

"As far as I know, just the eight I mentioned. Bay likes to call them his 'Circle of Faith.' That's Bay, of course; Morgan; Bay's wife, Elise; Meade; Roger Gillis, who runs the education program; Sam Reese, who they call Minister of Evangelism; his wife, Carola, a soloist with the choir; and Marley Wilkenson, who heads up the church's music program. Bay didn't want to get his board of trustees involved, at least not yet."

"How was your presence explained to others at the church?"

Fred frowned and slurped coffee, easing the cup back onto its saucer. "The church had some break-ins recently—nothing big, mostly just broken windows and petty vandalism. There's a night watchman, but he's older than Methuselah, and I don't think he hears very well. Anyhow, they did call the cops in on this, but they weren't much help, so the break-ins were a convenient reason to bring me in. And that gave me the excuse to ask all kinds of questions about anything relating to security—including how the dough's handled after the offering gets taken."

I've been around long enough to know when my boss loses interest, although others usually can't tell. I read the signs while Fred was talking, so I was hardly surprised when Wolfe held up a hand. "Would either of you care to stay for lunch? We're having shad with sorrel sauce."

"That's an offer it pains me to turn down, especially with the memories I have of past meals here," Parker responded with a sad smile. "But I must be in court at two. In fact, I should be going now."

"And I need to get home to Fanny," Fred said hoarsely. "When I called her after Mr. Parker got me out, she sounded worried sick." The truth in Fred's case is that he knows he's not overly welcome at Wolfe's table, and hasn't been since the day he asked for vinegar, which he proceeded to stir into a brown roux for a squab.

"Very well," Wolfe said, not sounding the least bit disappointed. "Fred, if you are able to spare the time this afternoon and can return, Archie has a number of questions." That was news to me—but good news, because it meant Wolfe was jumping in, fee or no fee. Not that I ever doubted he would.

FIVE

After lunch I hoofed it to our neighborhood branch of the Metropolitan Trust Company, where I had a certified check cut, made out to Parker for fifty grand. Back in the brownstone, I called Lightning Bolt Messenger Service, and within fifteen minutes, one of their kamikaze bicyclists—dressed in yellow spandex tights, black silky shorts and yellow jersey top, and black-and-yellow crash helmet—swung by and picked up the envelope containing the check, mumbling a vow that it would be on Parker's desk within the half-hour. I laid a healthy tip on the lad, then watched from the stoop as he pedaled the wrong way down Thirty-fifth Street, swerving to avoid a collision with a Yellow Cab, whose driver shook his fist out the window and yelled something I could not make out. It probably wasn't "Have a nice day."

I had time to get a batch of orchid-germination records entered into the PC before Fred came back to the brownstone at four-fifteen. The timing ensured he wouldn't run into Wolfe, who already was well into his playtime in the plant rooms. Fred looked almost as frazzled as he had earlier. "What does he think, Archie?" the accused asked as he dropped into one of the yellow chairs.

"He thinks—no, make that he *knows*—that you're as innocent as a newborn Lhasa apso," I said, swiveling in my desk chair to face him. "In fact, he's so sure of it that he's willing to commit my time to getting you cleared."

"What do *you* think, Archie?" Fred asked plaintively, avoiding eye contact.

"Oh, come on, for God's sake, remember who you're talking to. How long have we known each other? But if it makes you happy, I haven't forgotten how to ask direct questions: Did you plug Meade?"

"Hell, no."

"Okay, now that we've gotten that out of the way, let's move right along. First off, any nominations you want to make?"

He turned fleshy hands palms up and shrugged weakly. "No, but I gotta say that, for church people, a few of them didn't seem all that nice, especially Meade."

"Aha. Then let's talk about the late Mr. Meade— and the others. Start at the start."

That drew another shrug, no more lively than the first; Fred sighed and launched into it.

"Well, as I said this morning, I went to see Morgan a week ago last Saturday, the day after you gave him my name. We met in his office in the church, and he showed me the notes, the ones you'd already seen and sent back. Anyway, I told him the thing sounded tough, but that I'd give it a go. The pay was fine, I can't kick about that. Then Morgan took me in to meet Reverend Bay—it seems like a lot of the Silver Spire people work Saturdays—and that's when I learned that I couldn't be open about why I was there, except to that Circle of Faith bunch. With everybody else I talked to, I had to act like I was looking into the vandalism stuff."

For the next hour, Fred Durkin recounted his experiences at the tabernacle. I could feed you the whole thing verbatim, which is what Wolfe got later from me, but I won't, because most of it was unimportant. Here, though, are edited versions of Fred's comments about the big players at the big church:

Lloyd Morgan—"You've met him, Archie, so I know you've got your own opinions. To me, he's awful pompous and self-important. I doubt if he's smiled since Christmas mornings when he was back in grade school, if then. He acts like he's overworked, and, although he doesn't say it, he seems to disapprove of most of the others on the staff—except for Reverend Bay, of course. He acts like he's the only one of the staff who's concerned about Bay—not just the note thing, but Bay's overall well-being. And he looks worried all the time, shaking his head and tut-tutting. Must be a real stitch at a party. He was with some fund-raising outfit before he joined the Silver Spire."

Barnabas Bay—"Damned impressive guy. What you notice first is how young he looks. I did some checking later and found out he's forty-nine on his next birthday, but he could pass for thirties—early thirties. He's tanned, over six feet, and has sandy hair and a movie actor's jaw. Aside from all that, he's got a way about him that puts you right at ease; maybe it's partly the southern drawl. Anyway, as I told you and Mr. Wolfe when I was here before, he seemed more embarrassed by the notes than threatened. He said something like 'I think it's the work of some misguided and troubled individual, but Lloyd here, bless him, feels there might be some danger, so I've relented.' Then he stressed that he wanted my investigation to be very low-profile. I think he was saying it as much to Morgan as to me. The idea of bad publicity really spooks him."

Royal Meade—"Right after we'd been with Reverend Bay, Morgan took me to meet Meade and left us alone. Talk about instant dislike! I didn't take to him, and I know damn well he didn't like me. He is—was—a little younger than Bay, but he seemed older. Not a bad-looking specimen, but tense, you know, almost jumpy, eyes moving all the time. The first words out of his mouth to me were something like 'I'll be candid; I have no respect whatever for your profession, if it can even be called that. I'm seeing you only because Barney asked me to—and I know he did that because Lloyd talked him into hiring you. I fought the decision.' Meade went on to say he thought the notes were the work of some harmless crank and really didn't deserve the attention they were getting. Then he dismissed me—rudely, at that. And I found out later he was bad-mouthing me around the church, just on general principles."

Roger Gillis—"Gillis oversees the church's education programs, both for the adults and the kids. They must have three dozen different classes, some of 'em on weeknights. He's in his mid- to late thirties, but like Bay, he looks younger: lanky, loose, and with a big mop of red hair. He's a likable sort, the 'aw, shucks' type, you know? But underneath that easygoing way, the boy's as sharp as a small-town barber's razor. He doesn't miss much that goes on around him, and he seems to think those notes to Bay are worth worrying about, although he didn't seem to have a specific reason for feeling that way."

Sam Reese—"Reese has got the title Minister of Evangelism, which, he explained to me, means he's in charge of spreading the word and getting more people into the church, preferably as members. He's not much to look at—mid-fifties, a bigger gut than mine, and less hair than me, believe it or not. But he's a dynamo. He's played a big part in the church's growth, and he isn't exactly shy about saying so. Claims it was his idea to put billboards advertising the Silver Spire on the freeways years back, and he told me he provided the push to get Bay's ministry on TV. He also grabs the credit for setting up the shelters for women and the homeless, and for the newspaper and magazine publicity the church has gotten. As to the notes, he took Meade's position that they were the work of some crackpot. 'In a congregation as big as ours, you're bound to attract a few oddballs. It's the law of averages,' he said."

Carola Reese—"Sam's wife. She's at least ten years younger than her husband, maybe fifteen, which would make her fortyish or so. Mrs. Reese is the church's star soloist, met Reese some years back when she joined the choir. She's apparently been married before, but I don't know whether he has. She's borderline flashy, both in her clothes and the way she acts. I kind of like her, though—of all Bay's inner circle, she's the friendliest, or at least was toward me. As far as the notes, she felt they were worth worrying about. 'It sounds like someone with a sick mind' is what she said to me."

Marley Wilkenson—"Wilkenson's called Minister of Music, and he oversees the whole program—choirs, orchestra, guest artists, everything. The church's big deal is the 'Spire Choir,' which has made several best-selling religious records and tapes, like the Mormons out in Salt Lake with that famous choir of theirs. Marley's a wiry little guy, and has a head of white hair that would make Tip O'Neill jealous. He's a widower, and he's got a reputation for being tough, but no-body's about to knock his musical abilities or his success. He strikes me as a cold fish, though. He pooh-poohed the notes and said that worrying about them was just a waste of time."

Elise Bay—"Bay's wife, and what a beauty. I think she was maybe Miss North Carolina some years back. Once you get past the looks, which takes a while, you find out she's also got brains. When I met her, I fig-ured she was around the church a lot just because of who she's married to. Well, maybe that's how it started out, but I'm telling you, don't sell her short; Elise Bay is damn smart, she's got clout in the running of the place, and she knows how to use it. She acted decent enough to me, but I don't think she liked the idea of having a P.I. around. I asked her what she thought about the notes, and she was evasive, said they were an 'anomaly,' whatever that means. I got the feeling she wasn't losing sleep about them, though."

I leaned back and digested Fred's comments, then asked if he wanted something to drink. "I just want this nightmare to be over," he groaned, sagging in his chair and pressing his palms to his eyes.

"Understandable. But with Nathaniel Parker on the legal end and Mr. Wolfe on the puzzle-solving end, you haven't got any worries," I told him. That's me, ever the optimist. "Now, let's talk about last night's meeting, where everybody got so worked up."

Fred shifted in his chair, looking sheepish. "Well, I guess maybe I didn't handle it all that well, Archie. But, dammit, Bay wanted a report, and he got one. Apparently, he has these Circle of Faith get-togethers almost every Monday night; they're kind of informal, not like the church's regular meetings of officers. But because these are his closest advisers, he puts a lot of stock in what they have to say."

"And that includes his wife and Mrs. Reese?"

"From what I gather, they both are always invited. Yesterday afternoon, I was at the church poking around and talking to people on the staff, and Morgan told me that Bay wanted me to come to the Circle of Faith meeting at seven-thirty and fill them all in on my investigation. I told Morgan I needed more time, but he said to come anyway, and give a progress report."

"Then what?"

"What could I do? I went to the meeting."

"Details, please."

"Well, we were in the plush conference room on the ground floor—the same level as the parking lot. It's in the office-and-classroom wing, which itself is the size of a small office building. Anyway, Reverend Bay seemed uncomfortable having me there, but right after he gave the prayer to open the meeting, he turned to me and said something about how everybody around the table knew who I was and why I was present, which seemed unnecessary; after all, I'd had at least a few minutes with each of them over the last several days, and they all knew why I'd been hired. Then he asked me to summarize what I'd learned. I started slow, telling how I'd watched the services for two Sundays, how I'd used the vandalism cover when I talked to the office staff and others. Then I said I was sure the notes to Bay were an inside job."

"And all hell broke loose?"

Fred shrugged. "Yeah, you could say that. Meade jumped up and yelled he'd heard all the nonsense he was going to. He called me a 'sleazy snoop' and a few other things. That's when I made a big mistake."

"How so?"

"You know my temper, Archie. I have to work to sit on it, and the last few years, I think I did pretty good—mainly thanks to Fanny, who tells me to do things like count to ten and think good thoughts. This time, though, it got the best of me. Meade had been making smart-alecky cracks ever since I first walked into that place, and I finally popped. I told him off, using some words that should never get said in a church. 'Jackass' was probably the mildest one."

"Sounds like it fit him. What next?"

"Everybody looked shocked. Then Bay jumped in. First off, he led us all in a prayer, to cool things off, you know? I was dying to punch out Meade's lights, what with that damn smirk on his face, but I had to sit there looking down while Bay prayed, quoting something from the Psalms about how we should refrain from anger and wrath. Then he told all of us to find a room to meditate alone in for fifteen minutes, and we would reconvene."

"And you meditated?"

"Yeah. The building was pretty much empty that time of night, and I got pointed toward a small office nobody was using down the hall from the conference room. Most of the others went to their own offices, or found unoccupied ones."

"And that's when Meade was zapped?"

Fred nodded.

"Did you hear a shot?" I asked him.

"No, but I had closed the door of the office I was in. And Meade's was closed, too. Archie, that whole place is built like a battleship—they didn't stint on construction. Those doors are heavy and thick; they don't have windows in them, and they look like they're made of oak. You might not hear a shot through one door, and you sure as hell wouldn't through two."

"But it was your gun that did it?"

He leaned forward and put his head in his hands. "That's what the cops say. Go ahead and call me stupid, Archie; God knows, I've called myself that enough since last night. Ever since the first day I went to the church, I took to removing my suitcoat and hanging it in an alcove with a couple dozen coat hooks that's along that ground-floor hall. All the other men there—including Bay himself—work in their shirtsleeves, and I like to blend in as much as I can. But you know I always wear a shoulder holster when I'm working—like you do. I would have felt stupid walking around the halls of a church with a weapon sticking out of a damned harness. So I always hung up the holster and gun, and then draped my suitcoat over it so that all you saw walking by was the coat. I mean, it is a *church,* after all! Who'd ever think anybody would want to filch a gun there, let alone use it?"

"I can't argue with that logic. I probably would have done exactly the same thing," I said reassuringly. "Anybody else hang coats in that alcove?"

"No, at least not while I was there. They've got a small auditorium just down the hall, and I guess those hooks are used mainly when they're having some sort of function in the auditorium. The staff all probably hang their own coats in their offices."

"Do you know who might have spotted you using that alcove as a parking place for your trusty blunderbuss?"

Fred shrugged. "I guess anybody could have. To be honest, I didn't pay a lot of attention, though. I suppose anyone who noticed me come into the building could have figured out from the bulge under my suitcoat that I was carrying a gun."

"No doubt. How did you learn Meade had been shot?"

"Well, I'd been sitting in that stuffy little office for close to the fifteen minutes. Bay had asked us to do our meditating, but I was mainly thinking about what I was going to say when we all sat down again in the conference room. There was a knock at the door and Elise Bay came in, looking as pale as skim milk in a glass. She asked if I'd been sitting there the whole time—since Bay had dismissed us, that is. I told her I had. 'Something terrible's happened,' she told me then. 'Roy is—'

"I didn't give her a chance to finish the sentence. I was up and out the door. Meade's office is about thirty feet down the hall to the left of where I was, and both Morgan and Wilkenson were standing just outside his door, looking grim. As I walked toward them, Wilkenson held up his hand like a traffic cop. He told me to stop right there, that the police had been called and were on the way. As it turned out, Bay himself was inside, trying to administer CPR to Meade, which was futile. The guy had taken two shots to the head. Apparently, either one was enough to finish him. They found my thirty-eight and two shell casings from it on the floor in the office. Meade had been sitting at his desk when he'd been shot—from the front."

"Hard to make a case for suicide," I observed dryly.

"Yeah. And my prints were the only ones on the gun," Fred muttered. "I've been set up. Screwed."

"It sure looks that way. Who found Meade?"

"Wilkenson. His story is that he'd left his own office after fifteen minutes of meditating or whatever, and was walking down the hall toward the conference room. Said he came to Meade's door and knocked to tell him it was time to reconvene. He got no answer, knocked again, opened the door, and found the body slumped over the desk."

"Had anybody else emerged from their meditating places yet?"

"Wilkenson says no, that he was the only one in the hallway at the time."

"Mmm. And each of them had gone alone into a room?"

"Presumably. From what I could see, we all went into offices except Bay, who stayed in the conference room. Some—Meade, Morgan, Reese, Gillis, Marley Wilkenson—used their own offices. Those of us who didn't have an office, that would be the two women and me, got directed to other rooms."

"Who did the directing?"

"In my case, Meade. As we were leaving the conference room, Bay asked him to show me to an empty office—it's used by a membership secretary. And he told his wife and Carola Reese that there were a couple of other rooms down the hall that weren't being used. Apparently, nobody locks their offices."

"Trusting souls. Care to name a culprit?"

Fred gave me a helpless look, turning his palms up. "I wish I could, Archie, but I don't know what the devil the motive would be. For that matter, what's *my* motive?"

"Well, Meade was pretty rough on you, both in that meeting and earlier."

"Yeah, that's what the police said, and with the heat on them, they're looking for somebody to toss to the wolves, namely me. But both you and the cops know damn well that rudeness and name-calling don't constitute a motive for bumping somebody off."

"They do if you're a cop or a D.A. feeling the heat, as you just pointed out yourself. And what better target than a P.I. You know what slime we're supposed to be. And an Irish P.I., no less. You know what they say about Irish tempers—you made that comment about yours a minute ago."

Fred looked at me like a dog might look at the master who just kicked him. "That's a low blow, Archie."

"Hey, that's not me talking," I said, holding up a

hand. "I'm just parroting the law-enforcement mind-set."

"Thanks for cheering me up."

"Look, as I said before, you've got Wolfe and Parker in your corner, as well as your humble servant. Against us, the combined might of the N.Y.P.D. and the District Attorney's office doesn't have a chance."

Fred responded to my brave words with a weak smile. He knew he was up to his armpits in alligators, and so did I.

SIX

When Wolfe came down from the plant rooms, he found the latest edition of the *Gazette* folded neatly on his desk blotter. I'd been through it already, of course. The headline, in two-inch-high capitals, screamed MURDER IN THE CATHEDRAL! The secondary head, in only slightly smaller letters, read PRIVATE DETECTIVE CHARGED. There was a three-column picture of the Silver Spire tabernacle, and under it head shots of Bay, Meade, and Fred Durkin, along with a story that ran ten inches on Page One and jumped to the back of the first section, where it took up another two full columns. It didn't tell much that I didn't already know, except that the deceased was forty-seven and married to a Wall Street executive, had one child, and had been with the church since just after Bay founded it. Durkin was described as "a longtime New York free-lance private investigator, often employed by the legendary Nero Wolfe. In this instance, however, Durkin was operating independently, although he had been recommended to the church by Wolfe's associate, Archie Goodwin, himself a private detective."

An adjoining article by Tom Walston, the *Gazette*'s religion editor, described Meade as "second only to Barnabas Bay as a dynamic figure at the Silver Spire church. Insiders have said that Meade was clearly the anointed successor, if and when Reverend Bay decided to step down as spiritual head of the large and internationally known church and its affiliated television ministry."

I kept quiet while Wolfe read, and when he finished I gave him a verbatim report of my session with Fred, which earned me a scowl, nothing more.

"Any instructions?" I prodded after he had retreated behind his book. I didn't get an answer—not then, obviously not at dinner, and not when we were back in the office with coffee.

"Well, I suppose I'll have to stop in and see Fanny and the kids at least once a week, to try to keep their spirits up," I said. "Or maybe Saul and I can alternate. I'll take an orchid each time I go, to help brighten the place. I seem to recall that Fanny's partial to yellow, so maybe the *Oncidium varicosum* will be—"

"Confound it, what are you blithering about?" Wolfe set his book down and glared.

I answered the glare with raised eyebrows. "I was just thinking about what the Durkin household is going to be like after Fred goes to Attica. Even with Parker in his corner, he's a three-to-one shot to get life, of course, and I suppose—"

"Enough!" he bellowed. "Instructions."

So that is why, one fine spring morning a few days after Royal Meade's funeral, I was on the hulking ferry as it groaned into its slip at Staten Island. Part of my instructions from Wolfe was that I was not to go to the church until after the funeral because, he said, "The distractions among the staff will be manifest. They will be intense enough even the week after the services, but we can afford to wait no longer."

Before leaving home that morning, I had called the church for directions, and a chirping secretary had told me that "It's not more than twenty minutes' walk from the ferry terminal, and tours are every half hour." She'd helpfully given me street directions, which I copied onto a sheet of notebook paper I was now holding as I stood in front of the Borough Hall on Richmond Terrace, a street overlooking the waterfront and the distant towers of Wall Street.

"Downtown" Staten Island, if you can call it that, looks more like a small harbor burg than part of a borough of New York—a borough that, one, is tired of being a garbage dump for the rest of the city, and two, has of late been making noises to secede. Whatever the arguments pro and con, this sure didn't *seem* like New York. There were no horns honking, and only an occasional pedestrian on the sidewalks that passed in front of small, empty shops and more than a few boarded-up storefronts on one- and two-story buildings. If it wasn't a sleepy town, it was at least taking a breather.

After consulting the directions, I got myself squared away, heading south up Schuyler Street—and I do mean up.

If I ever knew how hilly the island was, I'd long since forgotten. In ten minutes, I was out of—and above—the small business district and into tree-shaded residential blocks where at least half the two-story frame houses cried out for a coat of paint and looked as though they had served as models for Charles Addams cartoons, complete with window shutters hanging at cockeyed angles by a single nail. I followed winding streets, all of which ran uphill, until, breathing hard, I reached a large open area that was level. In the center of this clearing, at least a block away, stood the Tabernacle of the Silver Spire, which looked vaguely like its photograph in the *Gazette*.

My first impression was "What's the big deal?" The blocky, glass-and-concrete hulk appeared unimpressive, but I later figured out that was partly because the spire dwarfed it. And, after all, I was still at least three football fields away. The "clearing" turned out to be a parking lot—acres of blacktop, crisscrossed with yellow lines. Poles supporting floodlights poked out of the asphalt at regular intervals. Each one had a sign with a section and aisle number, just like a shopping center, lest the worshipers forget where they parked the family sedan. As I walked across the lot, the tabernacle seemed to grow, and by the time I got to the entrance—four sets of double doors with silver, cross-shaped handles—I conceded that this was indeed a big deal.

I pushed into the entrance hall. It was twice the size of my old high-school gymnasium and had a chrome-and-gold chandelier that Donald Trump somehow missed when he was fitting out his casino in Atlantic City. A bright-eyed redhead in a snappy green outfit sat inside a circular, chrome-skinned counter under the chandelier and shot a smile my way. "Good morning, sir. Here for a tour?"

"Not today." I smiled back, recognizing the voice as the same one I'd heard when I called earlier. "I'd like to see Lloyd Morgan." My voice echoed off the walls, or maybe it was bouncing off the floor that made my footsteps sound like I was eight feet tall and wearing hobnail boots.

She asked if he was expecting me, and I shook my head but gave her my name and told her he knew me. She picked up her phone and punched a number. "Mr. Morgan, a Mr. Goodwin is here to see you. Yes . . . He says you know him. . . . Yes . . . All right." Cradling the receiver, she threw another smile at me, crinkling her eyes and showing off a pair of dimples. "Mr. Morgan will be out in a moment. You can have a seat over there, Mr. Goodwin." I smiled my thanks and walked around the hall, stopping to contemplate a large oil painting of Barnabas Bay in a chrome frame. The image oozed success and sincerity. Bay's blond hair was styled, his eyes looked bluer than the oceans on the big Gouchard globe in Wolfe's office, and his half-smile was all warmth and no smugness. I was still looking up at the face when clicking heels on the gleaming terrazzo floor announced Morgan's arrival. He obviously wasn't thrilled to see me.

"Why are *you* here?" he asked in an angry semi-whisper that couldn't be heard by the dimpled redhead. I noticed that he was wearing a silver lapel pin in the shape of the church's spire.

"To talk to you, of course, and Mr. Bay, too. I—"

"You've got colossal gall showing up after what's happened," he snapped, dispensing with the whisper. "I went to you in good faith, and when you and Mr. Wolfe turned me down, I trusted that your recommendation would be a sound one."

"My recommendation *was* a sound one, and still is," I told him. "Which is why I'm here. Fred Durkin didn't murder Meade, and Mr. Wolfe intends to find out who did."

"That's total nonsense!" Morgan hissed. "The police arrested him, it was his gun, and he—"

"Time out, please," I interrupted, holding up a hand. "You spent some time with Fred."

"Enough. He talked to me first, of course, when he came here. And we had a couple of other conversations, neither of them very long."

"And?"

"And what?"

"How did he strike you?" I asked.

Morgan shrugged and looked irritated by my questioning. "He was . . . all right, I suppose. It was clear that the man isn't a genius, but he struck me as a decent person. Which goes to show we all can be fooled at one time or another."

"He is a decent person, Mr. Morgan. I've known him for years, and seen him in some tough situations. Fred Durkin is *not* a murderer."

"Huh! The evidence is otherwise," he said stiffly. "Now, if you'll excuse me, I have a great deal to do."

"I'd like to see Bay."

"Impossible. He's tied up with a thousand things."

"Does he know I'm here?"

"No, but if he did, I assure you he would not want to see you. Now, if you'll excuse me, I'm late for a meeting." Morgan turned to go back to wherever he'd come from, and after a wave at the redhead, I fell into step with him.

"Mr. Goodwin," he said, wheeling on me and indulging in a deep, loud breath, "I must warn you that if you don't leave, I will ask one of our security guards to escort you from the premises. At the risk of sounding impolite, you are not welcome here."

"That's pretty impolite, all right. Okay, I won't tax the resources of your private constabulary, but you and the good reverend haven't heard the last of Nero Wolfe and me. So long." Having thus told Morgan off, I gave him a salute, but it bounced off his broad back as he stalked down the hall, presumably returning to his meeting.

So I'd been run off the property, sort of. Wolfe's instructions had been for me to try to see Bay, but not to push it. I sure hadn't pushed it, and I felt so frustrated that I barely smiled at the bright-eyed redhead in green as I went out the door. I started across the parking lot on my way back to the ferry terminal, when I spotted a cluster of people gathered outside another door to the big church. I put on the brakes when a woman in the group waved at me and said something I couldn't hear, so I got closer.

"Are you looking for the tour?" she asked when I was within a horseshoe pitch of her. "I'm about to start one."

I began to say no but put the brakes on my tongue. "That's exactly what I was looking for. Thanks," I told her. The guide was a pleasant-looking sixtyish lady with perfectly coiffed white hair, and wearing a tailored, buff blue sixtyish-lady's suit, and standing around her in a neat, respectful arc were eight tour-takers, six of them women. They all looked to be in the same age bracket as their guide.

"I thought you appeared to be a little bit lost," Ms. Guide said with an indulgent smile. "I'm Nella Reid, and I was just beginning to tell the rest of our guests here about how the Tabernacle of the Silver Spire came into being."

"Don't let me interrupt. Tell away."

"Oh, it's all right, I just this minute started. As I was saying to the others, our founder and leader, Barnabas Bay, began a ministry some eighteen years ago in a small town down along the New Jersey coast. He was young then—he's still young, in my view," she chuckled, "forty-nine on his next birthday. Anyway, Barney—that's what he likes us all to call him—had been an assistant pastor in two churches in Georgia, where he hails from, when he felt a call to come north. So he packed up with his pretty wife and went to this resort area just north of Cape May. For about four years, he preached to vacationers who would gather on the beach in the warm months; and he preached to the locals—there were a lot fewer of them, of course—in the cold months, using an old church building that had been vacant for ages.

"Well, the Lord works in wondrous ways. *Time* magazine heard about Barney, and they did a big feature on this 'barefoot preacher of the beach,' as they called him. After that article ran, money came in from all over, and Barney was able to build a beautiful new church building in that little town, a building that is still used today."

Nella Reid's eyes danced as she looked from face to face. "Now, if I were to ask each one of you to name the most godless city in America, what would you answer?"

A tall, big-boned guy with a deeply lined face and white hair falling over one eye who I later learned was named McPherson piped up: "That's easy—we're in it right now, the good ol' Big Apple."

"We're from Sioux Falls," his wife added solemnly, as if that lent weight to her spouse's opinion.

"Anybody else want to comment?" our smiling guide asked.

"I'd have to vote for New York as well," a moon-faced woman of a certain age laughed, "even if I did come all the way from Kentucky to see the town."

"I'll add my vote too," put in another woman, this one thin, with oversize dark-rimmed glasses and sporting a Prince Valiant haircut, "and I've been to Las Vegas—twice."

"Barney wouldn't be surprised to hear how you've all responded," Nella Reid told them in exactly the tone that Mrs. Cunningham, my third-grade teacher, used when congratulating one of us on spouting a right answer. "He felt, and feels, the same way you do. When he was down there in New Jersey, he knew the Lord was calling him to come to New York City, where there was—still is—so much work to do."

She paused, but she was nowhere near good enough an actress to make it seem spontaneous. "Now, I must add that New York is filled with absolutely wonderful, wonderful people, many of whom are stalwarts in our congregation. But there are so many more thousands who desperately need to be reached. Barney knew that when he came here fourteen years ago, and he knows it more than ever today, despite the magnificent progress he's made here at Silver Spire.

"See that?" she asked, gesturing dramatically to a small brick-and-frame church with a steeple about a fourth the height of the big spire in a thick grove of trees across the parking lot. "That is our Cana Chapel, and it was Barney's first building after he came here. He named it for Christ's first miracle, where He turned the water into wine at the wedding in Cana, because he felt his establishing a church on Staten Island—right in the city of New York—was indeed a miracle. We'll visit the chapel later, but now it's time to see the tabernacle itself. Follow me, please."

We obediently trailed her, with the McPhersons squabbling about what year they'd made their first and only other expedition to the wilds of New York. I think the wife won, but I made a point to drift to the opposite side of the group as we entered the building through a different door than I'd used earlier. Nella Reid led us into a two-story lobby and held up a hand to still any conversation.

"We are in the narthex of the sanctuary now," she said with reverence. "I know it looks terribly expensive, what with all this beautiful white marble on the walls and granite on the floor, but you should know that every bit of that stone—and most of the construction cost of the tabernacle and its office-and-school wing—was donated by a gentleman in the congregation who is a builder and who came to know God through Barney. Now let's go into the sanctuary."

It was an impressive auditorium, I'll give it that, with a big balcony and a wall of glass at least twenty feet high and twice that wide behind the pulpit that looked out on a grove of willows and a picture-postcard lagoon where a pair of white swans floated lazily. A large glass or clear plastic cross hung above the pulpit, apparently suspended on wires, although I couldn't see them. Nella told us, at least three times, that the place seated something over thirty-six hundred—all upholstered theater-type seats, not pews—and that it was jammed to the rafters for the three services Sunday mornings, plus one service each Sunday night. She pointed out the locations of the four TV cameras and the control booth at the back of the balcony where the sound and lights are monitored.

"Our middle service each Sunday is telecast on a cable hookup to more than two hundred stations across the United States and goes by satellite to several foreign countries. Barney preaches every Sunday that he's not traveling. And sometimes he illustrates his sermons with films or tapes," she told us proudly. "There's a control panel built into the pulpit that allows him to dim the lights, draw dark curtains electronically across the big window, lower the large screen that's recessed into the ceiling, and activate the projector upstairs. When we have a well-known singer or musician here to perform at a Sunday service, their image also gets projected by video on the screen so that worshipers farther back in the sanctuary get a better view."

"Real space-age stuff." Mr. McPherson of Sioux Falls nodded his approval.

"I guess you could call it that," our guide said. "We aren't trying to be fancy here, but Barney feels many churches today don't involve their congregations enough. He's always coming up with new ways to get his points across. For instance, you'll notice that the pulpit is actually up on a theater-type stage. Barney had the tabernacle designed with a stage rather than the traditional altar, because he likes the flexibility of sometimes having a playlet or a drama as part of the Sunday service. And the pulpit itself can be lowered hydraulically into the floor of the stage so that it's totally out of sight when not being used."

"Not what I usually think of as a church," said the moon-faced lady from Kentucky, shaking her head, "but I guess it must work."

"We like to think so," Nella replied, trying unsuccessfully to sound modest. "But we also know there are many paths to the Lord."

"Amen." That came from the Prince Valiant lady, the one who had been to Las Vegas twice. "Does Barnabas Bay work here during the week?"

Our hostess nodded vigorously. "Oh, yes, every day. We have a whole wing devoted to offices and to Christian Education—classrooms for both children's and adult Sunday school, as well as for classes that are held on weekday evenings. And we have a day-care center, too, for more than three hundred children."

"The offices—that's where that man who worked here was . . ." Mrs. McPherson, looking self-conscious and getting a stern eyeballing from her husband, let the sentence trail off.

"Yes." Nella pressed her lips together and studied her serviceable low-heeled black pumps. "That's where Mr. Meade was killed by that private detective. A tragedy, awful."

I started to respond to that trial-by-tour-guide remark, but stifled myself. Sobered at the mention of Meade's murder, we shuffled out of the huge sanctuary and moved on to the office-and-classroom wing. Nella showed us a couple of the classrooms, which would have made most universities envious, and as we walked along the hallway, a stunning brunette approached. "Hi, Nella," she said with a smile that could melt the polar ice cap. "How're those lovely grandchildren of yours?"

"Just fine thanks, Elise," she answered as the brunette moved fluidly away down the hall. Already my life seemed emptier.

"Who was that *beautiful* woman?" the Kentucky lady whispered, asking the question for all of us.

"Elise Bay, Barney's wife," Nella said. "And she's every bit as nice as she is beautiful. She's very active in the tabernacle's work. She was Miss North Carolina once, and from what's been said, she should have been Miss America instead of second runner-up, but, well, there were politics involved. You know how that can be."

We all nodded and continued on along the hall. I considered hanging back and drifting away from the group to do a little further solo exploring of the premises, but I took a pass. Wolfe has told me more than once that I lack patience, and after all, he had a plan. Or so he said.

SEVEN

B y the time I arrived back at the brownstone, Wolfe had finished lunch and was in the office with coffee and his book. Fritz, bless him, had saved me a plate of rice fritters with black currant jam, so I voted my priorities by sitting in the kitchen and polishing off the fritters, then chasing them with two wedges of blueberry pie before reporting. Besides, if I had gone straight in to see Wolfe, he would have refused to hear me out until I'd eaten anyway. If he had a motto, it would be something like "Food first, all else in due course."

When I did get to the office, carrying a cup of java, he was ready to listen. I gave him a fill-in, including my tour of the buildings and grounds. He kept his eyes shut throughout my report, scowling a couple of times and grimacing when I told him that Nella the tour guide had tried and convicted Fred. When I finished, he drew in air, letting it out slowly.

"Confound it," he grumped, ringing for beer, "get that minister on the phone." Wolfe always assumes I can reach anybody instantly just by picking up the phone, dialing, and declaring that Nero Wolfe is the caller. I punched the church's number, and the redhead who sits in the splashy lobby answered again. I asked for Bay, and she put me through without any questions.

"Doctor Bay's office," a pleasant female voice answered.

"Nero Wolfe calling," I told her, nodding to Wolfe, who picked up his instrument.

"What is this in reference to?" she asked politely.

"I think he'll know," I replied, and we got put on hold. For the next thirty seconds, we both were treated to the strains of "Holy, Holy, Holy," which for me brought memories of my Sunday-school days in Chillicothe. I'm not sure what it brought Wolfe, who doesn't like using telephones and likes hearing recorded music on them even less, but the hymn got interrupted in midverse by a voice only slightly tinged with a southern drawl. "Barney Bay here," it said. I stayed on the line.

"Mr. Bay, this is Nero Wolfe. I believe you know of me."

"I do indeed," the reverend replied evenly, "by reputation."

"I am drawing on that reputation to impose upon you, sir. I need to talk to you, preferably today."

"Well, I have a few minutes right now . . ."

"This conversation must be in person, and at the risk of further imposition, I request that it be held in my house, as I rarely leave it."

"I'm sorry, Mr. Wolfe," Bay said, his voice still even, "but I have a meeting in less than a half-hour, and I'm teaching an adult class here at the church tonight."

"Tomorrow, then." It wasn't a question.

I could hear Bay breathing, then sighing. "I assume this has to do with Roy Meade's death and your Durkin fellow."

"It does, sir, and it would be in the best interests of both you and your church if you spoke with me. I assure you I will not prolong the discussion unnecessarily. My time, like yours, has immutable value."

Another sigh. "All right, I can come tomorrow, in the midmorning. Ten-thirty?"

"Eleven," Wolfe corrected, then gave him our address. Bay agreed without enthusiasm.

"Okay, you've pulled it off," I said after we cradled our receivers. "I would've bet three-to-two against. Congratulations."

Although you'll never get him to admit it, Wolfe enjoys praise as much as the next guy. His mouth formed what passes for a smile, and he went back to his beer and his reading, while I swiveled to my desk, where orchid-germination records awaited updating.

The next morning, Wolfe beat Bay to the office, but only by half a length. It was precisely eleven when the groaning elevator announced the great man's descent from the plant rooms. He was crossing the sill into the office as the doorbell rang. "Get yourself comfortable," I told him, "while I play butler."

Viewed through the one-way glass in the front door, Barnabas Bay, clad in a light gray suit that made me want to ask the name of his tailor, looked surprisingly like the painting I'd seen twenty-four hours earlier in the tabernacle, right down to the warm-but-not-smug half-smile. He was alone on the stoop, although I could see someone behind the wheel of the modest dark blue sedan parked at the curb.

I opened the door and gestured him in. "Mr. Bay, I'm Archie Goodwin, Nero Wolfe's assistant."

"Oh yes, of course, Lloyd has spoken of you," he said in his gentle drawl, giving me a firm handshake. "In fact, he said you were at the tabernacle yesterday. Sorry I couldn't see you, but I had meetings all day. If I had known in advance . . ."

I told him not to worry about it, that I'd taken a tour. By then, we were entering the office, where I made introductions. Bay, who sensed Wolfe isn't big on shaking hands, nodded a greeting and eased into the red leather chair.

Wolfe leaned back and considered his guest. "Would you like anything to drink? I'm having beer."

"Ice water, please," Bay responded. Like Morgan, he had one of those spire-shaped pins on his lapel.

"Your given name is Robert Bailey," Wolfe went on after he'd touched the buzzer under his desk, summoning Fritz. "Why did you change it?"

If the question caught Bay off balance, he didn't let it show. "I'm afraid ministers are not without their vanities," he said with a shrug. I could see how he would project well on television. He had the looks, to be sure, and all his gestures seemed natural and fluid. "As a seminarian in Georgia, I grew to admire Barnabas very much. He worked closely with Paul in Antioch, and—"

"I am aware of who he was." Wolfe was taking the biblical lecture with his usual good grace. "A good man, full of the Holy Spirit and faith, and a great number of people were brought to the Lord."

Bay nodded, and his grin revealed teeth that could light up a revival tent. "Acts 11:24. You know your Bible well."

"It is literature," Wolfe responded. "Why the altered surname?"

"You seem very interested in my names," Bay answered good-naturedly. "I could tell you that I thought Bay seemed more dramatic than Bailey, which I suppose is partly the case. The main reason, though, is that my father deserted the family when I was eight. None of us ever saw him again. My mother raised four of us by working two full-time jobs, which probably took at least ten years off her life. I couldn't forgive him, and I didn't want to carry his name."

"Yet you are a highly visible representative of a faith in which forgiveness is among the most exalted of virtues."

Bay chuckled and slapped his thigh with a palm. "I like your direct approach, Mr. Wolfe," he said without resentment. "You are right, of course. My failure to come to terms with the anger I felt at my father has pained me for years. It's only recently that I've been able to work my way through it, at least to some extent. But," he added with a slight smile, "after all these years, I'm stuck now with the name I gave myself in seminary. I know you didn't ask me here to talk about my past, though."

"Indeed. Our business is very much of the

present. It is my intention to prove that Fred Durkin did not dispatch your associate."

"The evidence would seem to indicate otherwise," Bay said, lowering his voice theatrically.

"How would you describe your relationship with Mr. Meade?" Wolfe asked after giving Fritz Bay's drink order and requesting beer for himself.

"We were close, of course."

"One of the newspapers suggested that he was your heir apparent."

Bay folded his arms over his chest and closed his eyes for several seconds. I wondered if he was always onstage. "Mr. Wolfe, it's difficult for me to even talk about Roy right now, so soon after . . . well, so soon after what happened. And you can't believe all the newspaper and TV people that have been in the church the last few days. Lights and cameras everywhere. And of course the police. I wasn't even going to come here when you asked, but given that Lloyd approached you originally because of those notes, I felt that in a strange way I owed it to you."

"You owe me nothing, sir. But since you have raised the subject, what is your opinion about the origin of the notes?"

"My guess is, an eccentric. Sad to say, every church gets them once in a while. I even had a few back in my little parish in New Jersey."

"Have you received any other hostile missives since you've been in your present location?"

Bay looked at the ceiling as if in contemplation, then leveled his blue eyes at Wolfe. "Oh, just a handful, mostly complaining about the content of a sermon, or about the hymns we sang, or my theology. But never a whole series like this. And never so threatening. I suppose that's the underlying reason I agreed to let Lloyd come to see you. But honestly, they—the notes—didn't concern me much. I'm not easily frightened, Mr. Wolfe. And after all, we get more than twelve thousand worshipers at the Silver Spire every Sunday; a few of them are bound to be, well, *unusual*."

"What do you think of Mr. Durkin's theory that the notes came from someone on the church staff?"

"Unthinkable!" Bay snorted, waving the idea away as if it were a gnat. "That outlandish comment of his is what started the whole furor. If he hadn't said that, Roy would be alive today."

Wolfe drank beer and dabbed his lips with a handkerchief. "Was Mr. Meade in fact your designated successor?"

Bay calmed himself and shifted in the red chair while his television smile returned. "As I told that police inspector, Cramer, we'd never actually established a formal succession," he said.

"Was there a tacit understanding?"

Bay frowned and tilted his head to one side. "If so, it wasn't because of anything I said or did, although I can see where, given his duties, Roy may have made some assumptions. And possibly others made them, too. The truth is, though, I simply haven't started thinking about a successor. That's probably not good management on my part, but I'm not even forty-nine years old, Mr. Wolfe, and I feel like I have a lot of good years left in parish ministry, which to me is what the Silver Spire really is, despite our TV network and the national publicity and the books I've written." If that last reads to you like a rehearsed speech, join the club. That's how it sounded when he said it, too, although the guy really knows how to use his voice for maximum effect. I found I was almost enjoying hearing him talk.

"Assuming you were ready to step down, would Mr. Meade have been your choice as a successor?" Wolfe asked.

Bay waited several beats before answering, studying his hands and glancing at his elegantly simple wristwatch. "Roy has—had—been with me a long time. As Senior Associate Pastor, he functioned more or less as my chief of staff. He was loyal and devoted to our work—a real soldier for the Lord."

"But not a general."

Bay unleashed a self-effacing smile. "I didn't say that."

"You didn't have to," Wolfe remarked. "How did the members of your Circle of Faith relate to Mr. Meade?"

Bay took a drink of water, returning the glass carefully to the small table at his side. "Mr. Wolfe, Roy had many fine qualities. He worked day and night— in fact, I had to urge him to ease off sometimes, to go home to his wife and son. He was a fine preacher, with a strong delivery and well-prepared, well-organized sermons. He often filled in when I was away if we didn't have a high-profile guest minister lined up. And he always wanted everything to be just right— he was a perfectionist, which you must realize isn't always conducive to popularity."

"What comes to perfection perishes."

Bay raised his eyebrows. "That's not from the Bible; is it Shakespeare?"

"Browning," Wolfe said. "Have you in fact answered my question?"

An earnest nod. "As I'm sure you've gathered from what I've said, Roy tended to be rigid. Some of the others chafed at this from time to time."

"Did you intercede when there were differences?"

"Oh, Mr. Wolfe, indeed I did, indeed I did. Roy and I talked—and prayed—about his, well, I suppose abrasiveness is the best description. He was aware of the problem, and I feel he honestly tried to improve."

"But still you received complaints?"

A shrug of the gray-suited shoulders. "Occasionally."

"From whom?"

"Mr. Wolfe, we're getting into an area of confidentiality here," Bay said, rippling his brow. "I don't feel I can answer that."

"A man has been charged with first-degree homicide. I am not indulging in hyperbole by stating that his life is on the line."

"There is no death penalty in this state."

"Come, sir, that is a quibble. A long prison sentence spells the end for an individual as surely as does the hangman's noose or lethal gas."

"All right," Bay said, reaching for the glass of water. He did not raise it to his lips. "Every one of the Circle of Faith, and that includes even my wife, has complained at one time or another to me about Roy."

"What was the nature of the complaints?"

"Well, most of them centered on Roy's abrasiveness, as I mentioned before. He could be extremely curt with people. To give you a bit of background, I assembled the Circle of Faith as a somewhat informal advisory council, sort of like those 'kitchen cabinets' that presidents used to have years ago. All the people in the Circle have been part of the Silver Spire ministry just about from its beginnings. Elise, of course, has been with me a lot longer than that; we've been married almost twenty-five years. Anyway, the Circle has been extremely important to me, both as a spiritual support group and an advisory body. They're encouraged to be very close-knit and supportive of one another, as well as of me. Unfortunately, Roy tended to strain relationships, rather than bond them. He'd always been somewhat that way, and in the last several months, I'd gotten increasingly concerned about his divisive nature." Bay let out air loudly, as if exhausted by his short monologue.

"And you had told him of this concern?" Wolfe asked, draining the beer in his glass and contemplating the remaining foam sourly.

The clergyman's shoulders sagged. "Several times. And finally, about two weeks ago, we had a long meeting in my study. It got pretty tense. Roy just didn't seem to understand why I was so upset about his methods. He told me that I coddle the rest of the staff too much. Now, maybe I do try awfully hard sometimes to avoid confrontation, but that's my style.

"Mr. Wolfe, I'm a positive thinker, to lift the phrase from Norman Vincent Peale, and I don't apologize for being one. We call our approach at Silver

Spire 'Inspirational Theology,' which was also the name of a book I wrote a few years ago. Not a very exciting title, I admit, but it did sell pretty well, still does. Anyway, 'IT,' which is the abbreviation we like to use, calls among other things for everyone to place a high value on respect and support for one another. As a faith, we try to avoid confrontation and seek conciliation wherever possible. I loved Roy Meade, and I'll miss him terribly, both as an individual and as a brother in the Lord. But on too many occasions, his conduct ran contrary to our principles. He was always quick to find fault with others on the staff and point it out—both to their faces and, worse, behind their backs. More than once he made critical remarks—really critical—about one or another co-worker in front of others, including secretaries and even volunteers from the congregation who happened to be within earshot. Criticism given in the proper spirit is not necessarily a bad thing, as you know. But often Roy's criticisms were rough and, well . . . hurtful. And if the church leaders don't themselves set an example, then what is the flock to think?" Bay turned his palms up in what seemed like a gesture he'd spent time perfecting.

Wolfe looked peevish. "How long had Mr. Meade been affiliated with the church?" he asked.

"Since just after I'd come to Staten Island from New Jersey—almost fourteen years. Before that, we were in the seminary together, although he was a couple years behind me."

"What did he think of the notes?"

"He was even less concerned about them than I was," Bay replied. "He argued with Lloyd about bringing in outside help, said they—the notes—were merely the work of some crackpot and weren't something to worry about. We were in basic agreement on that."

"Regarding that serious conversation you had with Mr. Meade two weeks ago, what was the upshot?"

Bay replaced the water glass on the table, leaned forward in the red leather chair, and rested his arms on his knees, looking intently at Wolfe. "I told him that I felt he must—absolutely must—ease up in his management style and control his temper. The flash point was an episode Roy had with Roger Gillis. There had been some kind of minor foul-up in the scheduling of a new track of adult-education classes. It was not a big deal, really, but Roy acted like it was; he chewed poor Roger out in front of the membership secretary. Said something like 'We simply can't keep having screwups like this, or you can bet there'll be some changes made around here!' "

"Had Mr. Gillis been guilty of previous oversights?" Wolfe asked.

"Nothing major," Bay drawled. "Oh, from time to time he's been a little soft on details, but he more than makes up for it with his hard work and his good ideas. He's tripled the number of adult classes we offer in the last four years or so. And he's brought in a remarkable diversity of teachers—nationally known college professors, child psychologists, biblical scholars, and other theologians from the big schools in Manhattan. He even got the quarterback for the Giants to come over and talk on three straight Sunday nights about the role of faith in athletics. Of course, that really packed them in."

Wolfe was unimpressed. "You said you told Mr. Meade that he had to rein in his temper. If he couldn't?"

"We didn't get to that point. As I told you a moment ago, I try to avoid confrontation. I did tell him that we would start meeting more often, one-on-one, with a single agenda: talk about and pray about his . . . problem. And he vowed to try to do better."

"In the few days between that meeting and his death, had you seen an improvement in his behavior?"

"Honestly, no," the minister answered sadly, passing a hand over his blond hair.

"Sir, as you are aware, Mr. Goodwin went to your church yesterday and was denied admission by Mr. Morgan. Now—"

"I know, and I've already told Mr. Goodwin I was sorry about my not being able to see him then. We've all been a little edgy since Roy's death," Bay said. "And Lloyd was just being protective of me and the rest of the staff."

"I can appreciate that," Wolfe said, "and I also realize that Mr. Goodwin arrived on your doorstep unannounced. Now, however, I wish to make an appointment for him to return and talk to each member of your staff."

"That's asking a good deal," Bay said, sneaking a look at his watch. "I've already canceled two meetings and delayed another one to be here this morning. And my staff is upset and distracted enough as it is, what with the police and the reporters and TV people hovering around so much lately. And now you want to take even more of their time."

"Your concern for your employees is admirable, sir. In a very real sense, Mr. Durkin is an employee of mine, or has been on numerous occasions that span a far longer period than the life of your tabernacle."

Bay nodded and made a chapel with his long fingers. "And you remain convinced that Mr. Durkin is innocent—even though that innocence, if proven, would almost surely mean that someone at the Silver Spire is a murderer."

"Just so," Wolfe said. "But if you are convinced of Mr. Durkin's guilt, there is nothing to fear from having them talk to Mr. Goodwin. And as to time, I assure you he will not draw out the interviews unnecessarily."

"All right. I don't like the idea very much," Bay said, "but I'll ask each of them to make themselves available for Mr. Goodwin. I can't guarantee how forthcoming they'll be, though." He turned to me. "How soon would you want to see them?"

"Tomorrow," Wolfe dictated. "Preferably in the morning."

"That's awfully short notice," Bay complained. "I'm not sure they all will be in the building then."

"I'm confident you can arrange it," Wolfe said, rising. "If you will excuse me, I have a previous engagement." He walked out, leaving me to say the goodbyes to our guest, who watched Wolfe disappear with an expression somewhere between puzzlement and anger.

"He wasn't being rude just then," I reassured Bay.

"He's a genius, and when he has a lot on his mind, he tends to forgo some of the social niceties." What I didn't bother to tell him was that Wolfe's previous engagement was a trip to the kitchen to supervise Fritz in his preparation of the stuffed veal breast we were having for lunch. As if Fritz needs supervision.

EIGHT

The next morning at ten, I was back at the Silver Spire tabernacle after another ferry ride and another uphill walk that made my calves grumble. "Hi, you were here yesterday, weren't you?" my favorite red-haired and dimpled church receptionist bubbled with sunshine in her voice when I ambled into the lobby.

Pleading guilty, I asked for Bay. At the end of his visit to the brownstone, he had told me to see him before I started my round of interviews. "It's better if I prepare everybody first," he had said. "They're all pretty rattled by what's happened, which I'm sure you can understand. And when you come, I can tell you first what kind of reaction to expect."

I would have preferred a less structured and less publicized agenda, but since Wolfe had chosen to bow out of the discussion and poke around in the kitchen instead, I went along with Bay's suggestion. The receptionist punched a button on her phone, whispered something, then cradled the receiver with a smile that was as sunny as her voice. "Dr. Bay is expecting you. It's straight down that long hall," she cooed, pointing with a well-tended index finger. "Past the stairway and the elevator, and then on to the first door on your left. You can't miss it, or I should say them. They're actually double doors. They're beautiful—solid oak."

I thanked her, hoping she thought my smile was sunny, too. She was right about the doors; they looked like something out of a King Arthur book I used to read when I was a kid. The only things missing were the drawbridge and the moat. I pulled one of the doors open, stepping back into the present: a fluorescent-lit, gray-carpeted reception room peopled with two women at desks, both of them typing with a passion. "Mr. Goodwin?" the younger of the two said, giving me her own version of a sunny smile. "Dr. Bay is waiting for you. Please go right on in."

I opened another oak door, this one not quite as elaborate as its brothers, and found myself in a room about as big as Wolfe's office, with thick burgundy carpeting, bookshelves reaching to the high ceiling on two walls, and cream-colored draperies framing both windows. Bay looked up from behind a mahogany desk and nodded me to one of three upholstered burgundy chairs in front of it. His smile was partly cloudy.

"Mr. Goodwin, you're right on time," he said approvingly, leaning across the desk to shake hands. He was in shirtsleeves, his tie loosened. "I'm just tinkering with a sermon." He gestured to the computer on a table at his right hand. "Do you use one of these?"

I told him I did, and he favored me with a second approving nod. "Wonderful things, aren't they? Well, you're not here to discuss personal computers. I've talked to everybody in the Circle, and they are . . . willing to speak to you today."

"But not enthusiastic, right?"

Bay shrugged. "Given the circumstances, one can hardly expect enthusiasm. I had thought it would make the most sense for you to see Lloyd first. You already know him, and despite his attitude toward you yesterday, he seems pretty well reconciled to your being here now. For that matter, so do the others. But Lloyd's tied up in a meeting with our Finance Committee and won't be available until close to noon, so you're set to see Roger Gillis first—he's our Christian Education Director. I told each of them that you needed no more than a half-hour with them. Actually, I hope you can keep your sessions even shorter than that."

I said I'd do my best, and Bay picked up his phone, rapidly punching buttons. "Roger, Mr. Goodwin is here. Can you talk to him now? Good, he'll be right there."

Bay escorted me out of his study, and we walked a dozen paces down the hall. He knocked on another oak door, and we entered an office a third the size of Bay's. Fred had described Gillis as young-looking, but I was surprised anyway. The guy could easily pass for an Ivy League undergraduate, which is how he was dressed—herringbone sport coat, tan crew-neck sweater, checked shirt, khaki pants, deck shoes.

He popped up from behind his desk when we entered, coming around it to shake my hand. "Mr. Goodwin, I'm Roger Gillis," he said somberly before

Bay could make introductions. The director of education was maybe two inches taller than I, and probably fifteen pounds lighter, which made him downright lanky. His long, thin face went with the rest of him, and it was topped by a mop of carrot-colored hair that looked like too big a challenge for any comb, brush, spray, or mousse.

"I'll leave the two of you alone," Bay said, closing the door behind him as I took the chair in front of the desk that Gillis offered, while he sprawled in its twin. "I never like to have the desk between me and a visitor," he said earnestly. "It's like a wall."

I agreed and then started in slowly, asking Gillis about how long he'd been at Silver Spire and the scope of his job. I got brief answers, such as "nine years" and "I oversee all the education programs here, both adult and children's."

After five minutes of me asking questions and him giving clipped, curt responses, I held up a hand. "Look, you said your desk acts as a wall between you and visitors. Well, the desk isn't between us, but there *is* a wall, and you've built it. I know you're probably tired of answering questions. First it was Fred Durkin, then the police, and maybe some of the media, too—"

"Blessedly, Barney handled all the media contacts." Gillis sniffed.

"All right. You've still had to put up with a lot, and now there's me. I promised your boss I wouldn't take any more time than necessary, but you're not helping much."

"I've been answering your questions," he said defensively, running a bony hand through his hair.

"Barely. The faster I'm satisfied, the faster I'll be out of here."

Gillis cupped his narrow chin in his hand and frowned. "Mr. Goodwin, I'm talking to you only because Barney asked me to. Frankly, I see no reason for any of this. It's clear to everyone that Fred Durkin shot Roy. Now you come around trying to find a way to get your man off, presumably by implicating one of us."

"You're sure one of your number didn't shoot Meade?"

"Of course I'm sure!" His eyebrows shot up toward his hairline, and his jaw went in the opposite direction.

"Then what's to worry about?"

He frowned some more. "Well, I'd hate to see anybody try to fix things so that the blame somehow got shifted."

"The 'anybody' in this instance meaning Nero Wolfe and me. Mr. Gillis, unless one of you really is guilty, you hardly need worry. The police and the District Attorney think they already have their man. It would take overwhelming evidence to the contrary to get them to change their minds."

"And you're going to try to find that evidence," he said accusingly.

"If it exists. I'm sure that you as a church leader would not want to see an innocent person sent to prison for life."

Gillis's narrow face softened, and he nodded. "All right, Mr. Goodwin, you've made your point. I will try to answer you as fully as I can."

"Thanks. How would you describe the attitudes

of the members of the Circle of Faith toward Meade?"

He shrugged. "I can't really speak for any of them."

"Come on, you must have at least a general idea of their feelings. After all, you've been meeting as a group for years now."

It was clear from his tension that the guy was struggling with himself. After waiting several heartbeats, he made a sound somewhere between a sigh and a moan. "Roy was . . . not a popular person, you know. He could be pretty hard on others. Heck, I'm sure he was doing it because he wanted to see the church function to its full potential, but . . ."

"Yes?"

"Well, he had a way of getting people pretty riled up."

"Including you?"

The color rose in Gillis's face. "Maybe sometimes," he muttered.

"Care to give me a specific example?"

He studied his fingernails, then the palm of his hand. If he was looking for something, he didn't find it. "Well . . . it was at a Circle of Faith meeting a few weeks ago," he said in a drawl that was less pronounced than Bay's. I guessed he was from Tennessee or North Carolina, but I'm hardly an expert on southern speech patterns. "Roy had these figures on attendance at adult-education classes over the last several months, you know? The numbers were down, and he suggested that maybe the job had gotten too big for me, that perhaps it was time to get somebody in to 'give poor Roger here a hand,' as he put it so . . . well, so patronizingly. To tell the truth, he'd been bringing up this falling-attendance stuff for several months, but this was the first time he'd really gone after me."

"And the numbers were down?"

"Well, they were—are—but only fractionally. And over the last several years, they'd increased by double digits annually. It was inevitable that they'd level off at some point. For that matter, membership has leveled off, too. As a congregation, the Silver Spire has grown like Jack's beanstalk for ten years. You can't keep that up forever, and the same is true of church programs."

"But apparently Meade thought differently."

"Mr. Goodwin, Roy knew doggone well that it was unrealistic to expect unending growth in our education programs. We already had well over seventy percent of our adult members actively involved in one or more courses. I'll stack that up against any large church of any denomination in the country."

"Did he specifically single you out for criticism?"

"Not hardly. Sam—that's Sam Reese—took a lot of zingers from Roy, because like I said, overall church membership had leveled off, too."

"So what did Meade expect to accomplish by the criticism?"

Gillis nervously brushed his hair back from his eyes and leaned forward. "I'll tell you. He was trying to undercut everybody. Roy Meade was power hungry; he couldn't stand to see others get a lot of credit. He was number two on the staff, behind Barney, but he always wanted more. He—" Gillis stopped short. "I've said enough."

I waited until he wound down. "What did you

think about those notes that Bay had been getting in the Sunday collection?"

He shook his head. "I didn't like them, not one bit. Some of the others in the Circle figure they are harmless—you know, the work of some crank. But they worry me; there's a lot of mighty crazy folks running around nowadays. That's why I was glad when Lloyd talked Barney into getting a real investigator in here. Of course, look how *that* turned out. Why are you so interested in the notes, anyway?"

I countered a question with a question. "Don't *you* think the notes and Meade's death are somehow connected?"

Gillis shook his head vigorously. "No way, not at all. It's bad enough that Roy's dead—and I really do mean that fervently, regardless of what I said about him a minute ago. But there is still somebody else out there making threats to Barney. And believe me, Mr. Goodwin, I see them as very real threats. The evil's all around us."

"So it seems. How would you describe the meeting the night Meade was killed?"

"Nasty," he said, making a face. "Your Mr. Durkin said he was sure those threats were written by somebody here, which was bad enough. But then Roy started, well . . . *insulting* him, and then Durkin lashed back and said some awful things, really awful things. Barney led us all in prayer at that point, and then we had to go to our offices to meditate for fifteen minutes."

"And you came back here?"

He nodded.

"Where's Meade's office?"

"Across the hall and two doors down."

"Did you hear any shots?"

"No, but that's not too surprising, I guess. These are plaster walls, and I never hear any noises from the offices on either side of me. And you can see how thick the doors are, too."

"When did you first know Meade had been shot?"

"Sam Reese came in and told me."

"How do the others in the Circle of Faith feel about Meade?"

Gillis wrinkled his long nose. "Mr. Goodwin, I apologize if this sounds abrupt or rude, but I just don't want to talk about Roy anymore. Like I told you before, I've said enough, and I really must get back to work. I think Barney knows who you're supposed to see next."

I was getting the old heave-ho, but it didn't bother me, because I figured I'd gotten all I was going to out of Gillis, at least for the present. I went back to Bay's office, where the younger of the two secretaries was waiting for me.

"Mr. Goodwin, Dr. Bay asked me to take you down to Mr. Reese's office," she said brightly. "He's expecting you." I thanked her and learned her name was Diane as we went to the door right next to the executive office, which she rapped on. The muffled response sounded like "Come in," and I swung open the door. That's when I learned that my next interview would be with not one person but two.

NINE

They sat together on a beige sofa along the wall on the left side of the office, under a large framed color photograph of the church, sunlight gleaming off the spire. He looked pretty much like Fred had described him: paunchy, balding, generally unimpressive. And "borderline flashy" was a good description for her; she clearly was younger than her husband, although by no means a kid. I assumed her platinum hair—and there was plenty of it—had been artificially enhanced, but whatever the case, the end result was just fine with me.

A grim-faced Sam Reese made the introductions for both of them, while Carola dipped her head and gave me an almost-smile. "I know Barney said you preferred to see each of us individually," Reese told me after I took a chair at right angles to the sofa, "but we come as a team. That's the way it is."

His tone made it clear that there wasn't room for argument, so I nodded and forced a grin. "Fair enough; both of you know why I'm here, so there's no reason to beat around the proverbial bush. How did each of you feel about Royal Meade?"

"I don't know what that question's supposed to mean," Reese snapped. "How do you *think* we felt about him? We had all served together here for more than ten years. We were a close-knit group." Carola nodded what I presumed was her assent, although her face effectively masked any feelings she had toward Meade.

"All right, I'll phrase it more directly: Did you like him?"

Reese started to get up, but his wife eased him back with a hand on his arm. "Look, Mr. Goodwin," he said through clenched teeth, "the only reason we're putting up with this nonsense is because Barney requested it. Frankly, I find the whole business tasteless and objectionable."

"That seems to be the consensus hereabouts," I responded, "and I can sympathize with that position. But so that you know where I'm coming from, I find it tasteless and objectionable when someone gets falsely charged with murder."

"And you truly think your Mr. Durkin is innocent?" It was Carola Reese, her green eyes wide and her expression open and trusting.

"Yes, or I wouldn't be here."

Reese snorted. "Hah! You work for Nero Wolfe, which means you do what he tells you, regardless of what you happen to think yourself."

"Not so. It is true that I am employed by Mr. Wolfe, but I am my own man and always have been. I will be happy to supply references who are willing to attest to this, Mr. Wolfe among them."

"All right, let's get on with it," Reese said sourly. "You wanted to know if we liked Roy. Of course we did."

"Both of you?"

Carola opened her mouth, but before anything came out, her husband replied. "Yes, both of us, and—if I can be so presumptuous as to speak for others—the rest of the Circle of Faith as well."

"That's interesting. I had the impression Meade could be hard to get along with."

"I suppose almost everyone is, from time to time."

"And I also understand that he was on your case because of falling membership."

This time Reese did get up. His fists were clenched at his sides and the veins in his neck were standing out. "So that's out in the open, is it? Our Circle meetings are supposed to be confidential, but it's obvious they aren't anymore. Well, church membership is off, but only marginally, less than half a percent. And that's just for the last three-month period, hardly a trend." He paused for breath, and Carola tugged at his cuff. "Sam, sit down," she said soothingly. He did, still puffing, and she turned her big green eyes on me.

"Mr. Goodwin, my husband may not choose to say anything negative about a dead man, but I will. Roy Meade could be mean, petty, and—"

"Carola!" Reese yelped. "That's enough!"

"It's nowhere near enough, Sam." Her voice was quiet but steady. "No one has done more to build this church than you have, with the possible exception of Barney, and I do mean the *possible* exception." She kept those marvelous eyes fastened on me. "I've had to sit in these endless Circle of Faith meetings, listening silently while Royal Meade attacks Sam for one insignificant infraction after another. That is, when he wasn't attacking somebody else. The man was full of himself, an egomaniac. He couldn't stand to see anyone else get credit for anything. Mr. Goodwin, in case you're not aware of this, so much of the vision for what the Silver Spire is today came directly from this man right here."

"Now, Carola." Reese put a hand on her arm in a limp attempt to quiet her.

"Darling, he should know this," she said soothingly, stroking the back of her husband's fleshy neck. "It was your idea, nobody else's, to put up those billboards along the expressways and parkways for miles around advertising the church. That was really the beginning of our big growth period. And who came up with the plan to finance shelters for battered women and for the homeless? Certainly not Roy Meade, or even Barney, for that matter. And who pushed Barney to set up the TV network? I'm not sure he would have done it, at least not on the scale we have today, if you hadn't been so aggressive."

"Oh, I don't know about that," Reese muttered. He had kept his face down during his wife's little speech, but he had to be enjoying the lavish praise.

"Of course it's true," she insisted, giving me the wide-eyed bit again. "Mr. Goodwin, you asked if we liked Roy Meade. Well, maybe Sam did, but he's a far better Christian than I am—he always will be, and I love him dearly because of it. God may condemn me, but I honestly loathed Roy. He was—"

"Carola, please, I don't think you should go on," Reese told her sharply.

A tear rolled down one rouged cheek as she squeezed her husband's arm. "Maybe not, but I can't help it. This has been building up inside me for . . . I don't know, years, I guess. When Roy was killed, I was stunned—just as shocked as everyone else here. In a way, though, I was also . . . *relieved,* I guess. I know that sounds awful, but I can't help it. Believe me, I'm not proud of myself, but that's the truth."

"Who do you think killed Meade?" I asked her.

"We all know who did it!" Reese put in angrily. "Your man, that's who."

"Why would Fred Durkin want to kill him? They barely knew each other."

"I assume you're aware of that meeting we had the night Roy was killed, the one Durkin was at," Reese said. His face went crimson again. "The vitriol he displayed toward Roy—"

"Roy wasn't exactly pleasant himself," Carola interrupted. "He said some mean things, some really cruel things, about private detectives in general and Mr. Durkin in particular. I was really embarrassed by it."

Reese nodded. "I was surprised myself about how strong Roy came on. We all knew from the very start of this business that he was against having a detective brought in, of course. For that matter, so was I, although I wasn't as outspoken about it. Anyway, when Durkin made his ridiculous claim that those vile things were written by a staff member, I guess Roy simply had all he could stand. He really blew sky-high and said some pretty rough things to Durkin, who then sort of lost control himself and started using language that, well . . . shouldn't be used in a house of God. Or anyplace else, for that matter."

"That's when Bay said a prayer and had you all go off and meditate, right?"

"Yes," Reese said. "I came back here, and Carola went to one of the empty offices down closer to the conference room, right?"

"It's Edna Wayne's office—she's one of our membership secretaries. She isn't here at night," Carola told me. "And of course I don't have an office."

"Uh-huh. Did either of you hear any shots?"

They shook their heads in unison. "Mr. Goodwin, Barney didn't cut any corners when he built this place," Reese said. "Thick walls, thick doors. He didn't want anyone to be bothered by outside noises or distractions. To quote him, 'To do the Lord's work properly takes concentration, reflection, and prayer—all of which require peaceful surroundings.' We hear almost nothing from outside when we're in here with the door closed. And you know, Roy's office is right across the hall from mine."

"How did you learn about the shooting?"

"Marley Wilkenson came in all wild-eyed," Reese answered. "After the fifteen minutes were up, he left his office. There was no one in the hall, so he started back toward the conference room, and Roy's door was the first one he passed. He knocked, to tell Roy it was time to reconvene, and when there was no answer, he went in, and . . . well . . ."

"Elise ran in and told me," Carola said. "She was in an empty office across the hall from mine. She found out from one of the others, I don't know who."

"Back to those notes. Who do you think wrote them?" I asked.

"Lord only knows. Oh, those miserable, miserable little things—the start of all the trouble," Reese moaned, throwing his hands up and then letting them drop onto his knees with a slap. "Considering the thousands who come to church here every week, we're bound to get a few strange ones. And we do, from time to time. About two years ago, there was this woman who started showing up at our first service, the one at eight o'clock. Always sat on the main floor. She had to be at least seventy, poor thing, and to call her clothes ragged would be a gross understatement. Anyway, at the same time in the service every week, just before the offering was taken, she would stand up and shout 'Hallelujah!' three times. And I do mean shout. Believe me, she had a voice that would wake the dead in that cemetery a half-mile down the road. This went on for at least four or five Sundays."

"What did you do?"

"Turned out she was homeless," Reese answered. "Had been in a mental institution for years, but, like so many others these days, she'd been let out; apparently, there were no funds to keep her in there anymore. And she didn't have any family that we could find. Eventually, the church paid to have her admitted to another facility here on the island, a good one. She's still there; one of our ministers-to-the-homebound calls on her every week."

"But at least *she* was harmless, Sam," Carola insisted. "The sheets of paper are just plain evil."

"If taken literally," he conceded. "But I still think they have to be the work of some crank."

"Does Bay have any enemies that you're aware of?"

"Mr. Goodwin, if so, they've done a good job of hiding themselves. Now, it's true Barney will occasionally get a letter from someone, usually a TV viewer, saying he's not interpreting the Bible correctly, or that he is too liberal, whatever that means—they don't usually say. We probably receive, oh, twenty or thirty negative letters a year."

"But never anything like the six notes?"

"Nothing close. I think the strongest attack on Barney before this came from a woman in California who wrote him a number of years back saying that he was destined to go to hell because of his lack of a belief in the infallibility of the Bible. We never did figure that one out, because nobody holds the Bible in higher esteem than Barney does."

"Back to the notes. Neither of you has any idea who might have written them?" I asked.

Carola shook her head, while Sam raised his shoulders and dropped them, sticking his lower lip out. "Nope," he said. "I told you before that they must be the work of some crank. Why are you so interested in them, anyway?"

"Must be my natural curiosity," I said with a smile as I got up to leave. "Well, I appreciate the time you've both taken to see me. I'll continue my rounds now."

"I'm afraid that we haven't been all that much help," Sam Reese said, getting to his feet too. He didn't sound the least bit sorry.

"Quite the contrary. You've been extremely helpful," I replied to confound him, stepping into the hall and pulling the heavy door closed. As I pivoted toward the church office, I saw Lloyd Morgan striding toward me.

"Ah, Mr. Goodwin, this is good timing. I just finished a long session with several of the members of our Finance Committee. Grueling business, church finances. Most parishioners have no idea. Sorry I couldn't be here to greet you earlier." Was this the same guy I'd been stiffed by forty-eight hours ago? I started to comment on Morgan's about-face when he saved me the effort.

"You know, I was awfully rude to you day before yesterday, and I want to apologize. Chalk it up to tension, although that's no excuse, I know. Barney and I talked this morning, and we agreed that you and Mr. Wolfe are entitled to our full cooperation. After all, we—I—did come to you originally. And now, at least as an indirect result of that, one of your colleagues is in terrible trouble. Before we go on, have you been able to spend the time you've needed with others on the staff?"

I told him I had, and Morgan led me to his office, which was next to Reese's and was hardly shabby itself. He steered me to a brown wing chair that shared a cozy colonial corner with a lamp table and a slightly smaller yellow chair, which he fell into with a sigh. "It's good to be back in my own blessed little sanctuary. These money meetings always give me a migraine. Now, how can I help you, Mr. Goodwin?"

"To be honest, you probably can't," I told him, sinking into the brown chair. "But I'll do some asking anyway. How did you get along with Meade?"

"You *are* direct, aren't you?"

"My mother often lectured me on the merits of being straightforward in my dealings. She never liked what she called 'shilly-shallying.' "

He forced a chuckle, but the rest of his face didn't match the sound effects. "Yes. Well, I'm sure by now you know enough about Roy to realize that he was, well . . . something less than saintly at times."

"I did get the impression that he could stir the caldron of discontent."

"What a quaint phrase. Well, without for an instant questioning his dedication, I will say that he did his share of caldron-stirring around here over the years. Roy knew what he wanted, and more often than not he got it."

"Such as power?"

Morgan's flat black eyes studied me, then his onyx cuff link. "Power, yes, and also . . . visibility. Roy loved it when Barney was out of town—which was fairly often—and he could preach. He was a first-rate preacher, Mr. Goodwin. In some ways, he was almost as good as Barney."

"But not quite?"

He gave his cuff a tug, then exhaled. "No. His sermons were structurally sound and biblically based, the message was always clear, and his delivery was impressive, even riveting, more so sometimes than Barney's. But he lacked, well, warmth. Mr. Goodwin, he just plain didn't have warmth."

"And Bay does?"

"Oh my, yes. You are an extremely perceptive man, and if you'd ever heard the two of them in the pulpit, you'd sense the difference instantly. Barney has a gift few people are given."

"Getting back to you and Meade, how did you get along?"

Morgan leaned back and rubbed an earlobe. "Passably. It was clear years ago that we'd never be the best of friends, but we were always civil to each other."

"Was Meade critical of the way you did your job?"

I got a raised eyebrow and then a smile in response. "Oh, I get your drift," he said, nodding. "Let's see, who've you talked to this morning? Roger Gillis? Sam Reese?" I nodded.

He smiled again. "And it will be the same when you sit down with Marley Wilkenson, at least if he's candid with you. All three of them—Roger, Sam, and Marley—posed grave threats to Roy. Each one has a great deal of power within his own domain—education, outreach, and music. And Roy was jealous of anybody who had power."

"But don't you have power, too? After all, you're the money man around this place, right?"

That drew an honest-to-goodness laugh, close to a guffaw, from the stuffed shirt, and it sounded like something he should indulge in more often. "Mr. Goodwin, I may have some fiscal responsibility here, but in the first place, I am not an ordained minister like the other three, so I posed absolutely no threat to Roy's ultimate goal of running the Silver Spire—if indeed any of them did. Second, although you may think otherwise, given these beautiful facilities, money is not the engine that drives this church—faith and love are. I know that may sound hokey to someone whose life is immersed in crime, but it's a fact. Sometimes in Circle of Faith sessions and other staff meetings, when I raise concerns about funds, I feel almost like one of the money changers that Christ drove from the temple."

"Is the church in financial trouble?"

He looked at me like I was crazy. "Not at all! Not for one minute. We have extremely generous givers, and the cash flow is strong. But I still have these concerns from time to time about whether funds are being used properly. Nobody ever wants to hear what I have to say, though. They all seem to find any talk whatever about finances distasteful—and that includes Roy."

"But he didn't criticize your work?"

"I don't think he found it worthy of criticism. Basically, he was disdainful of my role here," Morgan said quietly. "To him, I was simply a pencil-pushing functionary."

"Who would want to kill him?" I asked.

He spread his hands, palms up. "Who indeed? Nobody that I can suggest. I'm afraid you're going to have to face up to the fact that Mr. Durkin is not only the prime candidate, he is the *only* candidate. He just flared up in that meeting and lost control of himself."

"About that meeting. I gather it was pretty ugly."

He cleared his throat. "I can't quarrel with that assessment. I'm sure you know the essence of it: Durkin said those notes came from inside the church, Roy lashed out at him, and Durkin lashed back. Durkin's language, by the way, is better suited to an army barracks."

"I can't count the number of times I've scolded him about it," I agreed. "Then Bay led a prayer and you all dispersed to offices."

Morgan nodded. "I came back here and honestly used the time in prayer and meditation. I had my head down on the desk, and the next thing I knew, Sam Reese came barreling in, telling me something terrible had happened."

"Let's go back to those notes to Bay—they were what got you worked up in the first place. How do you feel about them now?"

Morgan rubbed his cheek. "To be honest, I haven't thought about them at all since Roy was murdered."

"You said they were the work of a psychopath, somebody truly dangerous. Do you have any reason to change that opinion?"

"I don't know anymore, I really don't. Maybe Barney and some of the others were right. Maybe it was just some deranged individual." He coughed noisily and shook his head. "If so, Roy paid the ultimate price for my anxieties."

"Other churches in the area have been resentful of your success. Might somebody from one of them have written the notes, as harassment?"

That struck a nerve. "Mr. Goodwin, you're talking about fellow Christians!" he fumed. "I can't believe that any churchman would degrade himself that way. Besides, whatever anger there was about our success came in the first few years. Once we were established, the resentment—which was really exaggerated by the press anyway—died down, partly because we draw so many people from Manhattan and even farther away.

We haven't eaten into the attendance at nearby congregations all that much. I think it's been seven years, maybe even longer, since another church complained about the Silver Spire luring members away. In any case, the note problem seems to have gone away; there haven't been any for the last two Sundays."

"Might Meade have written them?"

He looked aghast. "That's really . . . absurd. What in the world would Roy have had to gain by doing such a thing?"

I shrugged. "After all, he wanted to run this place, didn't he? Maybe he figured he could scare Bay into an early retirement."

"I'm sorry," Morgan huffed as he got up, "but this conversation has taken an unpleasant turn. I wasn't close to Roy, but I don't wish to continue this discussion. It demeans him, and the Silver Spire as well. Besides, there isn't any more I can contribute to your investigation—if there ever was—and you've got others to see. Marley, right?"

"And Elise Bay."

"Oh yes, and Elise. I don't believe she'll be in till noon today, but Marley should be in his office right now. I'll point the way."

I couldn't think of anything else Morgan could contribute either, so I went out the door behind him, ready to face the man who makes the music.

TEN

Morgan couldn't get rid of me fast enough. When we were out in the hall, he gestured toward Wilkenson's office but made no effort to do any escorting, which was fine with me.

"It's the third door on the left, across from the main office," he muttered. "If Marley's not there, you'll probably find him in the choir room; one of the women in the office can give you directions."

I considered thanking him, but took a pass on that bit of civility. Besides, Morgan ducked back into his office so fast and shut the door that he wouldn't have heard me anyway. All by myself, I was able to find my way to a door that had a small brass MARLEY WILKENSON plaque engraved with musical notes. I rapped my knuckles on oak and heard something that sounded vaguely like "Come in."

Pushing the door open, I was in another well-decorated layout, this one done up in about ten shades of brown, from the carpeting and the walls to the draperies and the furniture and the lamp shades.

Wilkenson, his white hair as impressive as Fred had described it, sat behind a desk that looked as if it belonged in the Oval Office, scribbling furiously with a fountain pen the size of a small howitzer that probably set him back almost as much as his brown three-piece pinstripe. He looked up without expression. "Yes?"

"I'm Archie Goodwin; I believe Mr. Bay mentioned me to you."

"Yes, *Doctor* Bay did," he said, standing me corrected and fixing me with light blue eyes that were every bit as friendly as his voice. "Please sit down. Will this take long?"

"Not very," I told him, dropping into one of the two matching upholstered guest chairs—brown, of course—in front of his desk. "Just a few questions."

"Your 'just a few questions' is about all I have time for right now," he declared. "In fact, I don't even have that luxury, but after all, Barney did ask me to see you."

"I promise that I'll be brief. If I understand this operation correctly, you're in charge of all the music at the Silver Spire."

"You hardly needed a meeting with me to confirm that," Wilkenson said, smiling sourly.

"Just a feeble attempt to be sociable," I responded with an honest-to-goodness grin, my sincere one. "Did your job bring you into contact with Meade often?"

"Correct."

I waited for some more words, but they didn't come. "How did the two of you get along?" I asked.

"We each had our jobs," he responded sharply. "We rarely interfered with each other."

"How did you feel about Meade?"

Wilkenson sniffed. "What possible relevance can my feelings about Roy have? Or do I get damned simply by refusing to answer?"

"You aren't about to be damned by me under any circumstances," I said, rerunning my sincere grin. "The truth is, with my track record, I'd be hard-pressed to damn the devil himself."

That drew a real smile, which spread across Wilkenson's long, bony face and was joined by a chuckle. "I have to say I like your candor, Mr. Goodwin. Are you by any chance a tenor?"

"Beats me."

"I'm short a couple of first-rate tenors right now. One had the misfortune of being transferred to Philadelphia by his company, another decided to move to Colorado and to find himself, whatever that's supposed to mean these days." He snorted. "Well, you're not here to listen to my problems. As far as my feelings about Royal Meade, they were frankly ambivalent. Roy was an incredibly dedicated man—a real workaholic. It seemed like he was always in the office, early mornings, nights, Saturdays. And he was a good preacher, too. But that intensity . . ."

"What about it?"

He studied his handsome pen, then looked up at me and wrinkled a white brow. "Roy could never unwind—at least I never saw it. He was always in high gear, tense. Now, this is a big operation, Mr. Goodwin, as I'm sure you've noticed. But I don't think of it as a business—at least not like the businesses across the harbor." He made a vague gesture with a hand in the direction of Manhattan.

"But Roy was the only one of us, other than Lloyd, of course, who seemed like . . . well, a businessman rather than a churchman sometimes, if you follow me. He was—*hard*, there's no other word for it. And his people skills frankly weren't very good; he didn't have much patience with anything less than perfection— at least his definition of perfection."

"That can't have made him very popular."

"He wasn't very popular. Oh, on the surface everyone was rowing the same boat, but that's because most of the staff and the lay leaders of this church and the other members of the Circle of Faith are fine Christians who practice their faith. They tend to forgive breaches in manners and avoid confrontation. And everybody knew how much Barney valued Roy, so they didn't want to complain. A few of us did talk to Barney about him from time to time, though. As I mentioned earlier, I got along reasonably well with Roy—the music operations are in the main self-sufficient. But others have complained to me about his brusque and even insensitive attitude toward them. I felt Barney should know, so I mentioned it to him— without naming names, of course."

"Care to name names now?"

I got another ice-blue glare. "I do not."

"Tell me about the night of the murder."

"Good Lord, the papers and TV have been full of it! What's left to know? Fred Durkin all but accused somebody in the meeting—he didn't say who—of writing those blasted threats Barney was getting, and Roy came down on him like an anvil. Then Durkin blew his stack and started cursing, and Barney stepped in. We all went away to cool off for fifteen minutes, and you know the rest."

"You found Meade."

He snorted. "Correct. After fifteen minutes were up—actually it was a little longer than that—I got up and poked my head out in the hall. It was empty, so I figured, since other than Barney I was the farthest one from the conference room, I'd work my way back, getting everybody to return to the meeting. Roy's door was the first one on my side of the hall, so I knocked twice and got no answer. I opened the door, and he was . . . face down on the desk."

"Who do you think killed him?"

He sighed irritably. "Come, come, Mr. Goodwin. We're all indulging you with these cursed interviews. There's not a person under this roof right now who doesn't think Fred Durkin shot Roy. And, of course, that includes Barney. I commend you for your loyalty to a comrade in trouble, but it's a sadly misplaced loyalty. Do everyone a favor and give it up."

"Call me a lover of lost causes," I told him. "What do you think about those notes that Barnabas Bay got?"

Another grumpy sigh. "The work of some oddball. We get a few weird ones occasionally. That's to be expected considering the number of people who worship here every week. But I hope you're not trying to somehow tie those notes to Roy's death—that would be ridiculous. Now, I'm afraid you'll have to excuse me," he said, rising. "I have a meeting in less than ten minutes with the woman who oversees our Sunday-school choirs."

Never one to stand in the way of meetings, I got up, too, figuring I'd gotten about all I was going to out of Wilkenson, at least for the present. He walked with me to the door and shook hands, unsmiling. "I'd wish you luck, Mr. Goodwin, but in this case, I'm not sure what that would mean, so I'll just say good-bye."

I didn't much like the guy, but at least he was honest. I said good-bye, too, and returned to the main office, where only one of the two secretaries, Diane, was at her desk. "Oh, hi again, Mr. Goodwin," she said with a lilt, looking up from her typing. "I guess you've talked to Mr. Wilkenson now, haven't you?" I told her I had.

"That just leaves Mrs. Bay for you to see, right?" I nodded. "She's in the conference room, catching up on some paperwork. She said to just go right on in; she's expecting you. It's way down the hall, almost to the end on the left, just beyond the drinking fountain."

Thanking her, I went back along the corridor to yet another door—I'd opened almost all of them in the last couple of hours. Even though the plaque said CONFERENCE ROOM, I treated it as if it were a private office and knocked on the oak, waiting a discreet few seconds before pulling the door open.

I like to think I've been around enough beautiful women through the years that I don't behave like a stage-door Johnny anymore, but Elise Bay almost made me want to rush out to buy a dozen roses. Even though I had seen her once before, almost exactly forty-eight hours earlier, I wasn't quite prepared for the face framed in dark hair that smiled up at me from the conference table where she was sitting with papers spread out around her. Chances are she didn't hear the catch in my breath as I stepped in, every inch the sophisticated big-city detective.

"Mr. Goodwin," she said in a quiet, warm voice that had just a touch of the Carolinas in it, "please sit down. I apologize for the conference-room setting, but this becomes my office when I stop in three or four times a week."

I said I didn't mind a bit and slipped into a chair across from her, wondering what adjective would best describe the shade of gold in her eyes. I mulled that over while catching a scent from her that I didn't recognize but wouldn't mind getting more familiar with. "I didn't realize you had a formal position here," I said as an icebreaker.

She smiled and spread manicured hands, palms up, in a movement similar to one I'd seen her husband make. "Oh, I don't, not really. I guess I'm what you'd call an almost-full-time volunteer. I oversee the calling teams the church sends out to visit our homebound members, which means a lot of paperwork and a lot of telephoning." She gestured to the phone next to her. "Say, I've seen you before. Yes—on one of Nella Reid's tours of the church. Day before yesterday, wasn't it?"

I grinned. "You've got a good memory, Mrs. Bay."

"You're easy to notice, Mr. Goodwin."

"I'll take that as a compliment until I hear differently. And please call me Archie."

"It was meant as a compliment, and I'm Elise. Is that Archie as in Archibald, or as in Archer?"

"As in just plain Archie. Your husband told you why I'm here, didn't he?"

She nodded. "Yes. And I'll help if I can, although I really don't know how."

"First off, what was your opinion of Royal Meade?"

Her eyes moved around the big room, as if she was forming an answer. "That's a more complicated question than it sounds, Mr.—Archie. I had several opinions about Roy."

"I'm interested in all of them."

She gave me the same smile that probably turned Bert Parks's knees to jelly in Atlantic City years before. "Roy was a very complex person. I don't think any of us—even Barney—knew just how complex he was. First and most important, he was a tireless worker. My, what a worker," she said, throwing up her hands and shaking her head. "We all had a hard time keeping up with him. I never saw a man with so much energy, and believe me, Barney himself is no slouch in the energy department."

"There can be too much of a good thing," I said.

"Yes, and I'm afraid that was sometimes the case with Roy. He was so terribly, terribly intense. I think that's why he'd get carried away and get cross with people sometimes."

"You among them?"

Pink showed in her cheeks. "Once in a while. Roy was very detail-oriented, and I'm not really always as good on details as I should be. That irritated him occasionally, although it was really pretty minor. There was never what you'd call a real out-and-out argument between us."

"How did his irritation manifest itself toward you?"

She sawed her lower lip with TV-bright teeth and frowned. Even her frown was worth committing to memory. "You know, I'm probably blowing this up into too big a deal. I don't mean to make Roy out to be an ogre or anything."

"Believe me, you're not. Go on."

"Okay," she said, trying to smile. "I guess it's just that I'm a little nervous. I've never talked to a private detective before, and I'm worried about what to say."

"What's to be worried about? After all, the police interviewed you after Meade's murder, didn't they?"

"Yes, but they seemed so sure that Mr. Durkin had shot Roy, while you think it was somebody else—which would have to make it one of us, wouldn't it?"

I shrugged. "Maybe. You were starting to tell me how Meade showed his irritation toward you."

She cocked her head and shot me another smile. "No, I wasn't, Archie, but I will. Roy was clever about it, or at least thought he was. If we were in a meeting with other people, he would say something patronizing like, 'Given your schedule, I can understand how you might have overlooked such and such.' He did that all the time, trying to make it appear that I was spread too thin."

"Were you?"

"We have four children, although they're not really children anymore—two are in college, two in high school. But when they were growing up, I was at home most all of the time. I only came in here a day a week or so. Now they're gone and I have more flexibility. I serve on the board of one of the shelters for abused women that we support, and I'm in here three or four days a week. I don't see that as an overload."

"Why did Meade suggest that it was?"

She looked at the two-carat diamond on her left ring finger, and when she spoke, she didn't look up. "Roy really didn't want me on the staff at all, even as a volunteer, and I know it bothered him that I was part of the Circle of Faith, too. But he wasn't about to say anything that would bring him into a direct confrontation with my husband. As it was, Barney had been on Roy's case lately about the way he treated other staff members."

"It seems like Meade caused more trouble than he was worth," I observed.

"But he was an awfully good preacher," Elise said in a whisper, finally looking up. "And as I mentioned before, he did the work of a small army."

"It probably wouldn't surprise you to hear that what I know about churches wouldn't fill one side of a sheet in a loose-leaf notebook," I told her, "but I still don't see why your husband didn't go out and find himself a Number Two person who got along better with the rest of the crew. No matter how good a preacher and worker Meade was, you can't tell me he was indispensable."

She shook her head sadly. "No, no, I can't tell you that. Only the Lord is indispensable. Apparently nobody's mentioned what happened when they were in the seminary together."

"I have a feeling I'm about to learn."

"It's not something that gets discussed often. In fact, I'm not sure everyone in the Circle of Faith even knows about what happened," Elise said, still almost whispering. I wanted to reach across the table and give her hand a squeeze.

"This was a few months before I met Barney," she went on. "He was in his last year of seminary, that was down in Georgia, and Roy was two years behind him, but they'd gotten to be casual friends. On a long weekend or a break between terms, I forget which, they went to one of those Gulf Coast resort towns along the Florida panhandle that college kids like so much—Panama City, I think it was. Anyway, Barney, who never has been a very good swimmer, went out a little too far off shore and got caught in an undertow. Roy swam out and carried him in. Barney was unconscious—blue, the way Roy told it—and he gave Barney artificial respiration for a long time, by whatever method they used back then. A crowd gathered. Barney told me that the first thing he remembered when he regained consciousness was this mob of people standing around him on the beach. Roy was a hero."

"And your husband owed him his life."

"Yes," she said soberly, "and it's a debt that he's been paying off for almost fourteen years now, Archie. I don't mean to sound bitter, and I certainly didn't mean to go on this much. Forgive me."

"There's nothing to forgive. I assume your husband brought Meade in as an assistant because of this debt."

Elise ran a finger along one nicely arched eyebrow. "It was about a year after Barney got here, and all we had then was that small church building—we call it the Cana Chapel now—that you probably saw on your tour with Nella the other day. Roy came look-

ing for work; he'd had several positions since seminary, the last one as an assistant minister at a little
parish someplace in the Tennessee mountains, and it
hadn't worked out, something about a difference in
philosophy between him and the senior pastor. He
asked Barney for a job, and you can guess what happened."

"Barney couldn't say no."

"That's right," she answered, setting her jaw. "At
that point, we were just getting started here, and we
weren't in a position to afford another pastor, but as
you phrased it, Barney couldn't say no. I urged him
not to hire Roy. I reminded him they had never really
been all that close before the swimming incident, but
he went ahead anyway. He said he owed it to Roy."

"That decision couldn't have been too much of a
calamity, given the way the church has grown since
then."

She leaned back in her chair and let her shoulders
sag. She still looked dazzling. "I wouldn't call it a calamity, by any means. Roy played a big part in the
success of the Silver Spire," she said, "but . . ."

"But you never liked him."

Her shoulders sagged some more, making me
wish I could do something to perk her up. "No, you're
right. I hope I loved him, as one Christian loves another—I know I prayed for him regularly, and for all
the other members of the Circle of Faith and the staff.
But I never really liked him. And I *wanted* to like him,
I honestly did." She stopped herself abruptly and
looked up at me with an expression of surprise. "How
do you do it?"

"Do what?"

"Get people to talk. I haven't said as much about my feelings toward Roy Meade in the last ten years as I have today, except maybe to Barney, and then mostly indirectly. Then you come in here and hardly ask any questions at all, and I start spouting like Old Faithful."

"It's a trick I learned many years ago in the Orient," I said with a thin smile. "Now that I've got you gushing, tell me what happened on the night Meade was shot. The meeting was right here, wasn't it?"

She nodded, her eyes moving from one end of the big table to the other. "Right in this room. As I'm sure you know, the whole Circle of Faith was here. And Mr. Durkin, of course. I don't mean to sound like I've got ESP or anything like that, but I had a bad feeling about that meeting even before it started."

"Why?"

"I'm not sure. It wasn't those notes that Barney had gotten; they never really bothered me all that much, and I frankly thought bringing in a private detective to find out who wrote them was kind of silly. So the notes, or whoever wrote them, didn't frighten me. Any man in the public eye as much as Barney gets accustomed to dealing with cranks. I don't know, I just had a . . . *feeling* that something was going to happen."

"Who do you think wrote the notes?"

She chewed on her thumb and shook her head. "Somebody who was disturbed, obviously. We get some pretty weird people here occasionally. I don't know if it's because we are on TV and that draws them to the tabernacle, or what. I'm glad we're well-publicized—anything that brings folks to the Lord is good—even though you also risk, well, the kind of person who devised those horrid messages." She shuddered delicately.

"So I gather you don't see any connection between the notes and Meade's murder?"

"Good heavens, no. Archie, I know he's your friend, but I don't doubt for a second that Mr. Durkin killed Roy."

I leaned back and stretched my arms over my head. "But anyone in the meeting *could* have done it, right? There was plenty of time, while the rest of you were all closeted in offices meditating for fifteen minutes or so."

She frowned. "Technically, that's true, but in the first place, good Christians—and I certainly include everyone in the Circle of Faith in that category—aren't murderers. Second, why would any of them—any of *us*—want to murder Roy? And third, how would we even know where to find Mr. Durkin's gun?"

"Those are all good questions, Elise, and I can't answer them. But then, I'm not the question answerer on our organizational chart, I'm the fact collector. Mr. Wolfe answers the hard questions. All I can tell you is that Fred Durkin isn't a murderer, either. How did you learn that Meade had been shot?"

"From Marley Wilkenson—he burst into the office where I was; he was hysterical. He'd just found Roy."

"And you were in a vacant office?"

"It's used by one of the membership secretaries," she said. "And it's right next to Roy's office."

"But you didn't hear shots?"

A shake of the head. "No, but you really can't

hear *anything* through these walls. I remember sitting in Barney's office with him one time when Sam Reese, who was right next door, opened one too many drawers on his filing cabinet at once, and the whole thing tipped over and almost fell on him. Sam told us it made quite a thud hitting the floor, but we never heard a sound."

"Interesting. What did you do that night after Wilkenson told you about Meade?"

"I ran into Roy's office to see if I could help, but Barney was already there, giving him CPR. Then I went to other offices, telling Mr. Durkin and Carola what had happened."

"How did Fred react?"

"He was surprised—or at least he *acted* surprised. I remember asking him if he'd been in that room the whole time. I guess subconsciously I was suspicious of him, even then."

"Uh-huh. I'd like to go back to the notes for a minute, since they're what triggered everything else. They were found in the—what do you call them, offering pouches?"

"Yes, for six weeks running."

"What happens to the pouches after the Sunday services?"

"They're taken to the vault—that's in a room one floor below us—and locked up until Monday, when the counting teams come in and sort through the cash and the checks, which then get deposited in the bank."

"Is it a vault with a combination?"

Elise nodded. "Yes, a dial."

"Who knows the combination?" I asked.

"Each of us in the Circle of Faith, and nobody else that I'm aware of. But I don't see what that proves."

"It may not prove anything," I said as I stood up. "Remember, I'm just the fact collector. And I'm not even sure that the facts I've been collecting will be of any use to Mr. Wolfe. All I can do is feed them to him and let genius take its course. I know you've got a lot of work to do, so I'll leave you alone. I know the way out."

She looked up at me with a smile that again— just for an instant—made me want to rush to the nearest florist and buy a dozen long-stemmed American Beauties. There are probably a lot of guys around who send roses to other men's wives, but I don't happen to be one of them.

ELEVEN

It was almost three when I got back to the brownstone. Wolfe was in the office, and he looked up from his book when I walked in. His eyes said "Well?"

"Do I report?"

"Have you eaten?"

"No, I—"

"Confound it, empty stomachs make for empty minds, and I have concern enough for your mental capacity when your stomach is full. Fritz has saved you a plate of sweetbreads. We will talk at six."

Meaning when he came down from his afternoon romp with the orchids, which was fine with me. Wolfe and I are in agreement that Fritz's sweetbreads amandine in patty shells are worth a postponement of business. For the second time since the Tabernacle of the Silver Spire had intruded on our lives, I ate a late lunch at my small table in the kitchen, lobbing compliments Fritz's way, which always makes him blush. "How is the case going, Archie?" he asked, twisting a towel in his hands. Fritz worries when we don't have a job, and when we do have a job, he worries that we won't get paid.

"Moving along," I answered between bites. I wasn't about to tell him that this looked more like a *pro bono* enterprise every day. I made the sweetbreads and a wedge of apple pie disappear and carried a cup of coffee to the office, where I sat at my desk and played back to myself what I'd dug up. By all accounts, Royal Meade had alienated everybody in the Circle of Faith, in varying degrees. But, I asked myself, why would even his strongest antagonist at the church want to shoot the guy? Sure, he was a royal pain, to indulge in a cheap pun. So are thousands of other people, though, and they don't have bull's-eyes pinned to their heads.

I printed the names of the Circle members on a page of my notebook. There was the earnest, insecure, paranoid Roger Gillis, who was positive Meade wanted him tossed out as Christian Education Director. It was hard to imagine Gillis killing anything larger than a spider—a very small spider. But he had been publicly humiliated by Meade, which can sometimes turn the mild wild. I remember the "quiet, bookish" auto mechanic in Newark who made national news by running amok with an Uzi after his boss had chewed him out in front of some customers. Maybe Gillis, too, had been a stick of dynamite waiting to be lit.

And what about Sam Reese, the marketing dynamo who was bitter and defensive about Meade's trying to muscle him aside? He was an intriguing possibility; I didn't have to work too hard to visualize

Reese smiling as he pulled the trigger and watched Meade slump across his desk. But did he have the nerve—or the motive—to dispatch Meade?

Carola Reese looked like a more likely candidate from where I sat. For starters, she'd been around the course a few times before she and Sam paired up—that seemed clear. Second, either she was one hell of an actress or she was genuinely incensed about the way Meade had been treating her husband. I voted for the latter. I like a woman who goes to bat for her man, but what if her bat becomes a thirty-eight-caliber revolver? This one definitely was worthy of further research.

I penciled a large question mark next to Marley Wilkenson's name. To be sure, he was an arrogant number, and I don't like anybody presuming to tell me I've got a "sadly misplaced loyalty." But neither of those character flaws qualified him as a murderer. And to hear Wilkenson tell it, Meade pretty much kept his mitts off the music program. Something whispered to me, though, that there was more between those two guys than I was getting from Wilkenson. The question mark stayed.

Even though he had attempted to become our client, I wasn't about to eliminate Lloyd Morgan from consideration yet. True, he seemed too stuffy to even contemplate anything as drastic as murder, let alone committing the act itself. Also true, he didn't seem to have a whole lot of motive I could see for dispatching Meade. I put him down as a long shot.

That left the Bays. I opted to give the padre a pass, at least for the moment. It was bad enough that

somebody near the top of the church hierarchy probably killed a minister; I wasn't about to cast Numero
Uno as the villain—not yet, anyway.

Then there was Elise, stunning Elise. She didn't
like Meade, not at all—it didn't take somebody with
Wolfe's brainpower to figure that out. And it also
didn't take a genius to realize that beneath that wonderful exterior she had the strength of steel. Assuming that her loyalty to her husband was intense and
absolute, as it appeared, then anything or anyone
threatening his success would presumably be her
enemy, right? Right, but I still couldn't see Elise using
Fred's thirty-eight on Meade. And it wasn't because
she dazzled me, although she did. I've known a few
other beauties who've used handguns to solve their
problems, including one who I once thought might
make a dandy Mrs. A. Goodwin. But that's a story for
another time.

I looked at the list of names again, shaking my
head. Nothing fit. I toyed briefly with the notion that
maybe Fred Durkin really *did* pull the trigger, but
within seconds I hated myself for the thought. Fred
was no killer—in fact, he was too averse to violence
to even be in the business, which is probably why he's
never done all that well at it. His idea of a good time
is an evening of TV with Fanny and the kids, and he's
turned down some good out-of-town assignments because he doesn't like to be away from the family.

Only once that I knew of did Fred go after a man
with intent to kill, and I have good reason to remember the episode. Years ago, the owner of a trucking
outfit came to Wolfe and asked him to find out who
was hijacking cargo—mostly computers and other

electronic gear—from his rigs. Wolfe wasn't much interested, but the bank account was unusually anorexic at the time, and I nagged him into accepting the case. It ended up being more complicated than I had thought, and we hired both Saul Panzer and Fred to help stake out a warehouse and loading dock in Brooklyn where Wolfe and I figured the stuff was being lifted from the trucks.

One night Fred and I were there, both armed. The warehouse was a block square and as dark as the tunnel of love. Around midnight, I thought I heard something. I was right, but slow. I'd found one of the hijackers, or rather, he found me. I still remember the moment when the flashlight beam played on me. "Say your prayers real fast, because you're gone," he hissed, and I heard a shot and tensed, but didn't feel anything. The flashlight banged onto the floor, followed by moaning. When I got to the guy, he was lying there, clutching his right arm. His sleeve was beginning to show a stain, and his pistol was next to his open hand.

I leveled my Worthington on him and played my flashlight cautiously around the warehouse. Fred came barreling into the halo of light, panting, his own gun drawn. "You okay, Archie?"

"Yeah. Did you fire?"

"Uh-huh, once."

"My God, what a great shot! You nailed him in the arm."

"Not so great, Arch," he wheezed, looking at the hijacker as he writhed on the floor. "I was trying to kill the bastard."

Okay, that's a long way of saying it, but Bay wasn't

the only one around who had a big debt outstanding. I was still scolding myself for thinking even for an instant that Fred might have shot Meade, when the phone brought me back to the present.

"Oh, Mr. Goodwin—I'm glad I caught you in." Carola Reese sounded tense. "I need to talk to you."

"This is as good a time as any. Go ahead."

"No, I mean I . . . well, I need to *see* you. I'd rather not talk about this over the phone. I'm in Manhattan—at the ferry terminal. I can meet you anyplace you say, as fast as a taxi can get me there."

I thought about having her come to the office, but figured Wolfe could walk in on the middle of our conversation. She sounded nervous enough as it was, and having him around wouldn't help that any, to say nothing of what it would do for his disposition. He tolerates women in the brownstone, but only when there's absolutely no alternative.

I looked at my watch. "Tell you what. It's four-thirteen. There's a coffee shop at Twenty-ninth and Third, southwest corner. It's quiet, it's clean, and it's got booths. I'll meet you there at, say, quarter to five. That should give you plenty of time."

She thanked me more than was necessary, and I hung up, going to the kitchen to tell Fritz I had an errand but would be home for dinner. Fritz did not greet the news with enthusiasm. "Archie, you are away for too many meals," he said as soberly as if I'd just told him a relative had died. "That's not good."

Assuring him I was not about to miss his lobsters with white-wine sauce, I ambled into the outdoors. The skies had turned gray, but I bet against rain and walked, heading east on Thirty-fifth. At Third, I made a right turn, landing in the coffee shop at twenty to five. Carola wasn't there yet, so I took a booth near the door and ordered coffee.

I was on my third sip when she walked in wearing mauve-framed sunglasses and looking as though she'd just landed in a country where she didn't speak the language. Then she saw me and took a breath, smiling. "Thank you for seeing me on short notice," she said, sliding in across from me. "I hope you aren't angry."

I grinned. "I save my anger for bigger calamities, like the Mets' bullpen and cabbies who don't know how to find their way from Herald Square to Rockefeller Center. Now tell me, what is the agenda for today's meeting?"

She smiled weakly. "I feel very stupid about this, but I don't know what else to do. I guess I should start by saying my life hasn't always been, well . . . lived right, if you know what I mean."

"Mrs. Reese, I have yet to meet anybody whose life has always been lived right."

"That's nice of you to say, Mr. Goodwin," she replied, drinking from the cup that had just been set in front of her. "But in my case, I really mean it. Really. Before I started coming to services at the Silver Spire, and then met Sam, I was on the wrong track, in a lot of ways."

"Why are you unloading now?"

She looked down at her coffee, pulled off the big sunglasses, and aimed green eyes at me. "Because of what Roy Meade said to me."

"You've got my attention."

"This is hard to talk about, but I knew this morning, when you were with Sam and me, that you were somebody who would . . . listen. I don't know anything about Mr. Wolfe, but you—I don't believe that you are judgmental."

I couldn't think of a suitable response, so I didn't say anything. She allowed a smile to escape, this one first-rate, and then went on. "After Sam and I got married—that was almost six years ago now—I felt like I'd been given a second chance. And the truth is, I had. It really started when I joined the Spire Choir, not long after I became a member of the church. I've got a good voice, Mr. Goodwin; I was a nightclub singer for years—here, the Poconos, the Catskills, even a couple of the smaller spots out in Vegas. Which gives you some idea of the kind of people I was hanging around with in those days."

She stopped for breath and more coffee, and the cup shook in her hand so much that I thought the java was going to spill onto the table. "Anyway, you don't want to hear all this stuff. I—"

"I want to hear whatever you choose to tell me."

That earned Doctor Archie another smile. "I'd been singing with the choir for, oh, maybe three months when I met Sam," Carola said. "It was at a coffee-and-cake reception in the main lounge after one of our Sunday-afternoon choral concerts. He'd been a widower for about four years, and—well, things just developed, you know?"

I nodded. "What about Roy Meade?"

"Oh, yes, what he said to me. Well, about a year or so after Sam and I got married, Barney formed the Circle of Faith. I was surprised that he asked me to be part of it. I figured it was just because I was Sam's wife, and I told Barney that it was a nice gesture, but I knew it was Sam that he really wanted in the group.

" 'No, Carola,' he said to me, 'I want you there, too, every bit as much as I want Sam; your faith journey is an inspiration, and don't ever, ever sell yourself short because of what you may view as a tarnished past. The life experiences you've had give you a far better perspective on the world than many people—and I believe those experiences have strengthened you greatly in your Christian walk.' So I became part of the Circle, and I could tell almost from the first Circle meeting that Roy resented my presence there, although I didn't know for sure why."

"Did you ever ask him?"

She shook her head. "No, I've always gone out of my way to avoid confrontation. But I thought maybe it had something to do with my marrying Sam. Roy had known Sam's first wife, and I figured maybe I didn't measure up to her. Or that maybe he disapproved of the kind of life I'd lived before I found the Lord, which I guess would be easy to understand. Anyway, Roy and I hardly ever spoke to each other, except for the occasional 'Hello, nice weather, isn't it?' kind of pleasantry. And then, about eight months or so ago, I was stuffing envelopes for a mailing in one of the unoccupied offices—I do volunteer things like that around the church a couple of days a week, whenever they need an extra pair of hands. The door to the office was open, and Roy was walking by in the hall. He looked at me, and then came on in and shut the door behind him."

"A little unusual, wasn't it, given your relationship with him up to that point?"

"Very, and it startled me. He came over to my desk and looked down at me, very solemn, frowning. 'How are you and Marley getting along?' he asked. I didn't understand where he was heading, and I said something like 'Just fine.'

" 'I'll bet it's just fine,' he said with a terribly nasty tone to his voice. 'Poor, poor Sam.'

"Then, of course, I got his drift—sometimes I'm a little slow—and I stood up and asked him, loudly, what he was talking about. I was shaking and trying to keep from crying. He just smiled—smirked—and walked out. It was awful."

"For the record, what is your relationship with Marley Wilkenson?"

She nodded grimly. "A fair question. Marley's a wonderful choir director—tough, but excellent. He really knows his stuff. And our relationship is strictly director to singer, that's all. I don't mean to sound like I'm bragging, but he was delighted to have me in the choir. First off, I'm good, and second, he has never had to pay me, which is great for his budget. The Spire Choir has a lot of paid soloists, but not me. I'm Mrs. Sam Reese, which is all I really want to be now, and I'm happy to sing—and solo—as a volunteer."

"Did you tell your husband what Meade said?"

Carola looked away from me. "No . . . never. Like I said, I don't handle confrontation well, and I didn't want to upset him. And I'd do anything to keep from hurting him in any way."

"Would he have believed you?"

She held her cup with both hands and allowed her eyes to meet mine. "Yes, I'm . . . almost positive that he would have," she said quietly. "And I did think about bringing it up, but I took an indirect tack instead. I asked several times if he thought I was spending too much time with the choir, and he always said something like, 'No, no, not unless you feel stressed out.' He loves my being in the choir. He's very proud of me and my contribution."

"Did Meade ever say anything to Wilkenson similar to what he told you?"

"Not that I know of. If so, I can't imagine Marley keeping as quiet about it as I did. He probably would have read Roy the riot act, then gone straight to Barney to complain about him."

"And nobody else ever knew about what Meade said to you?"

"I don't think so, although I was always worried about it getting out—even though there was really *nothing* to get out."

"Why do you feel Meade said what he did?"

She shrugged and shook her head. "I honestly don't know, except that he really wasn't a very nice person, and . . ."

The sentence trailed off as her glance went over my shoulder. I turned to see a tall, broad-shouldered guy with a forest of curly black hair lumber into the grill. He looked as if he'd been overserved, and he blinked twice as he noticed Carola. "Well, I'll be damned," he slurred. "If it's not the ol' torch singer herself. God, I haven't laid eyes on you in years, honey. You look great."

"Hello, Derek," she replied listlessly.

"You don't sound real happy to see an old friend,"

he told her, leaning on the table and grinning, then tossing a look my way. The atmosphere around the booth had quickly turned eighty-six-proof.

"Derek, this is Archie Goodwin. Archie, Derek MacKay," she said.

"Don't bother gettin' up, pal," MacKay said, slapping a beefy palm on my shoulder. He turned back to Carola. "So, I heard someplace that you went and got hitched up to a preacher-type over on Staten Island. This him?"

Carola cringed and obviously wanted to crawl under the table. "No, Archie is a friend," she murmured.

MacKay guffawed. "He don't look to me like a preacher. Oh, I get it, baby. You got yourself both a husband *and* a friend now. Pretty nice deal."

I shot him my best scowl. "Tell you what, Derek, why don't you go back outside and get some air? Mrs. Reese and I have some things to discuss."

Another guffaw. "Oh, so her name's Reese now, eh? And I'll just bet you two have got stuff to talk about. Good stuff. How'd you get so lucky, pal?"

"Pal, you started in on the joy juice pretty early today. It's time for you to leave," I told him, standing up. He had two inches in height on me, and probably at least that much in reach. But he was tanked, and that gave me a false sense of security. When his right came, I wasn't fast enough, and the fist caught me on the left cheek, knocking me backward. A couple at the next booth and an old guy on a stool got up and moved to the rear of the room, while the waitress stared from behind the counter, her mouth open.

I grabbed MacKay's right arm and in one quick

twist had him in a hammerlock, just like the book says to do. He howled and called me a couple of colorful endearments, and I pushed him toward the door. "We're going out to see what the weather's like," I said, moving him ahead of me as the filth kept spewing out of his mouth.

"I can either see how far your arm will go before it breaks," I told him when we were outside, "or I can let loose of it and you can walk away, just like nothing happened. But if I do let go and you try something stupid, you'll be lying on the sidewalk faster than you can say your favorite naughty word. What's the choice?" I gave his arm another upward yank, just in case he needed reminding.

"God, all right, I'll go, I'll go!" I dropped his arm, and damned if the lumbering oaf didn't come at me with another right, a roundhouse. This time I was ready. I blocked it easily and caught him on the chin with a right, following it with another right to the stomach, which doubled him over. I was ready for more, but he just clutched his gut with both hands, groaning. Our one-round bout had drawn a small but noisy crowd. Give New Yorkers something they want to see, and they'll turn out for it.

"I know, you're going to tell me that if you'd been sober, you would have put me away with three punches, four at the most," I said. "I'm willing to admit that's a possibility, but unlikely."

He swore again and straightened up, gritting his teeth and glaring. Whatever effect he was trying for didn't exactly come off, and he staggered off down Third Avenue, still swearing.

Carola was on her feet when I went back into the

grill. "Are you all right?" she asked tightly. "Oh, you're not—look at your face!" She dipped a napkin into her water glass and touched it to my cheek.

I flinched and smiled. "Hey, this is part of the reason Mr. Wolfe pays me so much." I noticed that the other customers had left the place, and the waitress was staring at me like I had German measles.

"Oh, I'm so sorry," Carola said, pulling the napkin away gently and grimacing at the small red blot on it as we sat down again. "He—Derek—is one of those people I told you about before, from my old life. I hadn't seen him in years; I didn't even know he lived in New York. It just shows that you can't run away from your past mistakes. They'll always catch up with you somehow."

"I don't buy that, and neither should you. I seem to recall something from my Sunday-school days about forgiveness for sins. How do you know MacKay?"

"He was a bartender at one of the places up in the Catskills where I used to sing. He was always asking me to go out, but I never had much use for him. Even then, and that was close to ten years ago, he was a bad drunk."

"Yeah. Well, he hasn't gotten any better. Ever see anybody else from your old life?"

"Never—this was the first time since I've been married, and I hope the last."

I dabbed my cheek with another napkin. It was tender, but the bleeding had stopped. "Getting back to Meade, why do you think he said what he did to you?"

"I honestly don't know. Before Derek walked in,

I started to say that Roy really wasn't a nice person, but then, you already know what I thought about him from when you talked to Sam and me."

"I seem to remember the word 'loathe' being mentioned. Is there any chance Meade made some remark to your husband about you and Wilkenson?"

She contemplated her fingernails. "I don't think so," she answered deliberately. "I think Sam would have told me about it."

"But you did not tell *him*."

"No."

"Even though you were positive he would have believed there was nothing between you and Wilkenson?"

Tears formed in Carola's eyes, and she started to shiver. "Oh, I guess maybe I was worried about how he'd react. I mean, he knows all about what my life was like . . . before. So do all the others in the Circle. I've talked about it, and except for Roy, they've been very supportive and understanding. But I'm still very self-conscious about those years. I just have never felt like I'm as good a person as the others."

"Why did you *really* choose to tell me about Meade's nasty little comment?"

She wiped her tears with another paper napkin. "I suppose I was worried that it might come out from somebody else."

"So you really were suspicious that he had talked to others about you and Wilkenson."

She sighed, and a tear spilled out of one of those jade-green eyes. "I guess so," she whimpered. "There's something else, too."

"Yes?"

"Years ago, I had a child. I wasn't married, but the father was, and he had no interest at all either in me or the baby. In fact, he was willing to pay me to keep quiet about everything. I didn't want his money, though; he was really a bad one, Archie. Of course, I was hardly a bargain myself." She stopped for breath and a sip of now-tepid coffee.

"Anyway, I put the baby—it was a little girl—up for adoption, and I have no idea where she is today. She'd be fifteen on her next birthday. Now, *this* part of my life I never told anybody at the Silver Spire about, not even Sam. I just couldn't bring myself to. But Roy Meade found out about it."

"How?"

"This is my year to run into so-called old friends. I said it never happened before, but actually Derek MacKay is the second one. The father of my child climbed out of his hole in the ground about six weeks ago. He saw my picture in a feature one of the smaller local papers did on the church choir. He's not married anymore, and he needs money, so . . ."

"So he's a blackmailer?"

Carola swallowed hard. "He wrote a letter to the church, addressed to 'Senior Pastor—Personal.' And wouldn't you know, Roy was the one who opened it. Barney was away at the time on a combination vacation and evangelical crusade to Australia, so Roy was handling all his mail."

"I'll bet Meade loved getting that piece of correspondence," I said.

"He did," Carola agreed glumly. "He came running to me with it. It was asking for five hundred dollars, as a 'consideration for maintaining a discreet silence about an event that could embarrass the Golden Spire church.' The jerk, Kyle is his name, couldn't even get the color of the steeple right. To say nothing of the fact that nobody with any brains would try to blackmail a *church*. Me, maybe; the church, no way."

"Kyle sounds like a real sweetheart. What did Meade say when he showed you the letter?"

"He could hardly hide his glee. He made a big, pompous deal out of telling me how he hadn't showed it to anybody at the Spire, and wouldn't. He said he was going to take care of things with Kyle, but he smirked the whole time. And then—God, how I hated Roy Meade—he said, 'Let this be a lesson to you, Carola. I, of course, believe in forgiveness, just as our Lord does, but I must tell you, I'm having a hard time believing you have turned your back on your past transgressions. One misstep of any kind on your part, and I will have to consider what to do with this letter.' What Roy Meade didn't know, Archie, is that not even Sam was aware of what had happened all those years ago. If Roy had known, he would have made life even more miserable for me."

"Did you ever figure out how Meade 'took care of things' with Kyle?"

She shook her head and stared at the tabletop. "Honestly, I think he could have just scared the guy off. Like I said, Kyle is a real jerk, or at least he was when I knew him, and the letter sounds like he hasn't changed one bit. But also, I think he's basically a coward. My guess is that Roy intimidated him somehow. I never wanted to ask. That letter, which Roy showed me but presumably kept, bothered me plenty. But it bothered me a lot more that Roy Meade had a sort of hold on me, and he could use it anytime he wanted to."

"But what would he use it *for*?" I asked.

"I'm honestly not sure. He never came on to me, if that's what you're suggesting," Carola said bitterly. "I really think he just liked having power over people. He was a manipulator; he always wanted control."

"Did you kill Meade?" I kept my tone conversational.

She jerked upright, knocking over her mug, which had less than a thimbleful of coffee in it. "Of course I didn't!" she hissed in a loud whisper. "Or else I wouldn't be telling you this." She looked at me as though I'd just slapped her.

"Sometimes guilty people talk a lot," I responded. "Maybe to throw their questioners off track. And—"

"So you don't believe me?" Carola wasn't whispering anymore, which meant we once again were the center of attention in the grill. She started crying again and began to slide out of the booth.

"I didn't say I don't believe you," I corrected her, holding up a palm. "Has that letter from Kyle been found among Meade's effects?"

She looked down again and began making circles on the Formica with a manicured index finger. When she finally opened her mouth, the "No" was almost inaudible.

"It probably wasn't hard to locate, was it?"

She lifted her head slowly, fixing me with eyes that held no warmth. "What does that mean?"

I grinned. "Don't let my youthful looks fool you; I may appear to be only a few years removed from my Eagle Scout badge, but I've been around the block a few times, and not necessarily to help little old ladies cross the street. Was the letter from Kyle in Meade's desk?"

She clearly wanted to be someplace else—any-place—but she stuck it out like a trouper. After some fiddling with her empty mug, she brushed hair back from her forehead and fixed me again with those marvelous green eyes, which now were warming up. "Yes, it was in his desk," she said, making a stab at smiling. "I waited until after the police had made their search of Roy's office. They really didn't spend much time, if any, going through his stuff. I guess because they knew they had the right man."

"I guess. Did it take you long to find the letter?"

She blushed. Nobody likes to be found out as a snoop, regardless of the reason for the snoopery. "Not really, no. I figured it would be in one of his desk drawers, not in a filing cabinet. I was right. Two days after Roy was murdered, I got to the Spire early in the morning—I told Sam I wanted to rehearse a solo. I found the letter in less than fifteen minutes, tucked away in a stack of miscellaneous papers."

"Where is it now?"

She smiled, but there was no joy behind it. "Where else? I destroyed the damn thing, tore it up in little pieces and threw it off the Staten Island ferry."

"I suppose I could make a citizen's arrest on charges of harbor pollution," I told her, "but I'll pass. Okay, if the letter is gone, why bother even telling me about it? Sounds like your secret is safe unless Kyle works up the nerve to write another little missive."

"Maybe Roy made a copy," she said hoarsely.

"A possibility," I agreed. "Still, why tell *me*?"

She nervously fiddled with her hair. "Because I had to tell someone, if just for my sanity. And unless I'm very wrong, you're used to hearing people's secrets—and keeping them. As I said before, I don't think you're the type that goes around passing judgment on people."

I smiled. "Maybe I should charge by the half-hour for therapy. Okay, so you've unburdened yourself to me. Now what?"

"Now . . . at least I feel better," Carola responded with a smile of her own.

I studied her well-arranged face, trying to figure out how much to believe. After a few seconds, I suggested we go, leaving the waitress a healthy tip to compensate for the business that got driven away by my sparring with MacKay. It didn't alter her dour expression any, though; some people just can't take a joke.

When we got outside I flagged a cab for Carola, and as I opened the door, I assured her she was every bit as good a person as anyone else in the tabernacle. She smiled but looked doubtful. Quite possibly she was considering the source of her assurance.

TWELVE

I walked back to the brownstone, climbing the front steps at six-twenty-five. I hit the buzzer, knowing Fritz would have put the chain lock on the door. He answered on the second ring.

"Your face," he said as he pulled the door open.

"Fritz, you have a wonderful knack for stating the obvious."

He frowned as I crossed the threshold. "But your face, Archie—it needs attention."

"I repeat my comment," I told him, marching to the office, where Wolfe wrestled with the London Sunday *Times* crossword puzzle.

He looked up and grunted. "Your face," he said.

"It must be this house. I've been back for all of thirty seconds, and the only two people I've encountered greeted me with the words 'Your face.' I think I'll go to the plant rooms to see Theodore. He almost never speaks to me except to gripe about something, but maybe he'll say, 'Your face—I recognize it.'"

Wolfe scowled. "Perhaps Inspector Cramer is correct when he insists that you will clown your way to the grave. What happened?"

"I ran into a fist, but only once. The other guy wasn't as fortunate."

"Indeed. Get cleaned up, and then report."

I went to my room and analyzed the damage in the mirror. A spot on my left cheekbone the size of a half-dollar had turned plum-colored. I soaked a washcloth in cold water and held it on the spot for sixty seconds, then dried it gingerly and covered the area with a bandage. When I got back to the office, Wolfe had defeated his puzzle and was hypnotizing himself by watching the bubbles rise in his beer glass.

I dropped into my desk chair and turned to face him. "Okay, here it is from the beginning," I said, giving him a verbatim report on the last eight-plus hours, from my arrival at the Silver Spire to my mini-scrap with MacKay and my hailing a taxi for Carola Reese. He kept his eyes closed and his fingers laced over his center mound the whole time, never once commenting.

After a half-minute of silence, to which he contributed nothing of genius, I went on. "It did seem kind of funny, Carola running into the guy after all those years."

He twitched his shoulders, which constitutes a shrug. "Perhaps, but she did mention she rarely comes to Manhattan. Encountering Mr. MacKay may indeed have been happenstance. Do you think that she and Mr. Wilkenson maintain a purely professional relationship?"

For years, Wolfe has been absolutely unwavering

in his belief that I can penetrate the deepest recesses of the female mind. He's wrong, but after all this time I hate to disillusion him. "It's about even money," I answered, "with maybe a slight tilt toward their having a little something going. She seemed too anxious to deny it."

He closed his eyes again. "Well," I said after another half-minute, "what now?"

"It is dinnertime. Lobsters in white-wine sauce." One thing about Wolfe, you always know what his priorities are. We did what we were supposed to with Fritz's lobsters while I heard a monologue on why the railroads were the greatest single force in America's westward expansion during the late 1800s.

When we were back in the office with coffee, I asked Wolfe if he had any instructions. He muttered something that sounded vaguely like "None" and opened his book, *Labor Will Rule,* by Steven Fraser. I was in the process of giving him a strongly phrased retort when the doorbell rang. "I'll get it," I said loudly. "Maybe it's a prospective client, wanting you to find her lost Chihuahua that broke loose from its leash on Beekman Place."

Our visitor was Inspector Cramer. "Come in," I said warmly, pulling open the door. "We were just getting ready to play mumblety-peg on Wolfe's desktop with a Swiss Army knife, but golly, we can do that any old time."

"You're a real gas," Cramer snorted as he lumbered in and made for the office. "What happened to your face?"

"I was afraid you wouldn't notice. I accidentally

wandered into the path of a little granny on Roller-blades who was heading for the spring clearance sale at Macy's."

I can't report on whether that drew a smile, because Cramer's back was to me as he chugged into the office and plopped down in the red leather chair. Wolfe looked up from his book with raised eyebrows.

"Yeah, I wonder why I'm here, too," Cramer said. "If I wanted comedy, I could sit home with my feet up and watch the cop shows on TV instead of listening to your court jester here." He jerked a thumb in my direction for emphasis.

"I agree that Archie's humor is often thread-bare," Wolfe said, exhaling. "I've spoken to him about it repeatedly, including tonight. It is a trial."

"Yeah, well, believe it or not, I didn't come to discuss Goodwin's pacing and timing. I want to know what's going on with the Durkin business."

Wolfe drank beer. "I know Fred has been charged with murder. Have there been further developments?"

"Oh, balls, stop playing around! You know damn well what I'm talking about. Goodwin spent more than four hours today at that religious monstrosity over on Staten Island. Somehow I don't believe he was praying."

Wolfe flipped a hand. "Archie's visit to the church should not surprise you; I stated earlier our intent to determine the identity of Mr. Meade's murderer."

"Uh-huh. And what have you found?"

"Candidly, not enough to make an accusation."

Cramer huffed. "I'm not surprised, given that the right guy's already been nailed."

"No, sir, that is not true—I know it, and you know it. If you were convinced of Fred Durkin's guilt, you would hardly tie up the valuable time of one or more of your men having them tail Archie."

"Damn straight," I put in to show that I was offended. I also was irked that I hadn't spotted my shadow at the Silver Spire. I wanted to ask Cramer if one of his grunts had seen me TKO MacKay on Third Avenue, but I passed on that.

"All right, so we had somebody on Goodwin," Cramer shot back, pulling a cigar out of his pocket and jamming it into his mouth. "I don't trust you as far as I can throw you, especially when it comes to saving the skin of one of your own."

"Come, Mr. Cramer," Wolfe said, moving forward in his chair and waggling an index finger, "if you are suggesting we would attempt to shift blame for murder to an innocent individual, you are riding the wrong highway."

"That's the only way you'll get Durkin off."

"I think not. And I am presumptuous enough to seek your aid. I was planning to telephone you tonight with three questions. First, have your men conducted a thorough search of Mr. Meade's office?"

"Funny you should mention that. As a matter of fact, one of our guys found something interesting at the bottom of a stack of papers in one of his desk drawers: photocopies of those six poison-pen notes that were sent to Bay."

Wolfe raised his eyebrows. "Your reaction?"

Cramer ran a hand through his hair. "Could be Meade was trying to get his boss to opt for early retirement so he could take over the operation."

"Indeed, sir. Do you really believe he was the author of those notes?"

"Look, we found out from others at the church—and I assume Goodwin did, too—that Meade was one poisonous customer, and damned ambitious. But if you're trying to tie the notes to the murder, forget it. You had other questions?"

"Have you spoken to Mr. Meade's widow?"

"Rowcliff talked to her at home—a house on the island about a mile from the church. She's with a brokerage firm on Wall Street, has a big job there. Anyway, Rowcliff said she's a pretty strong cookie, that she was standing up well. She told him she couldn't understand why anybody would want to kill her husband—which is what they all say, of course. But he didn't get much more out of her, although he wasn't trying all that hard, given that Durkin was already in the slammer. Apparently Meade enjoyed his work, so his wife said, and he put in awfully long hours. But what's the big deal with that? So do I. Look where I am at nine-thirty on a weeknight."

"When you could be at home watching police adventures on your television screen," Wolfe murmured. Humankind never ceases to astonish him.

Cramer glowered at his mangled cigar as if he'd never seen it before. "Yeah, right. I assume you're going to stick with this business. I've been around you long enough to realize that there's no way on God's earth I can pry you off something you've glommed onto. By the way, who's paying you?"

"No one," Wolfe replied.

"Incredible. That's one for Ripley. Well, if you

come across any information that I'd be interested in—and I'm just saying *if*, I'm not expecting anything—I want to know about it."

"That is a fair request, sir."

"I thought so too. What's your third question?"

"Have you conducted tests to confirm that a gunshot could not be heard from outside Mr. Meade's office with the door closed?"

"We have. That place really is a fortress. One of my men fired blanks from a thirty-eight in that office, and the guy out in the hall said he heard something that could have been a book—a small book—falling on a carpet, that's all. We also had people in the offices on either side of Meade's, and they didn't hear *anything*—not a peep. Before I go, you'd better damn well hear this, both of you," Cramer said, getting up and standing at Wolfe's desk. "Because Durkin is cooked, really cooked."

"You know very well that I prefer conversing with those who are at eye level," Wolfe growled.

"I'll keep standing, thanks," Cramer growled back. "The exercise is good for your neck. Anyway, here's two things maybe you don't know: First, the department up in Albany that licenses you guys got a letter about ten days ago from one Royal Meade of Richmond County—that's Staten Island, in case you were home sick the day they covered that in geography class. The letter, with a carbon copy to Durkin, said that he, Durkin, was unfit to hold a private investigator's license in the state of New York and went on to detail some of his tactics at the Silver Spire—including his bullying two women to let him see personnel records of various employees. As it turned out, they both refused to show him the records and told Meade about it.

"At the state's request, I sent a man to the church to check on Durkin's activities, and another woman on the staff, a part-time secretary, told my man she overheard Durkin saying 'I'm going to kill that bastard' after he and Meade had had a noisy argument in the hallway outside Meade's office."

Wolfe raised his shoulders and let them drop. "Angry braggadocio on Fred's part," he remarked.

"Yeah, well, how do you think it'll play in court when that nice little woman—she's about four-eleven and in her sixties—quotes Durkin?"

"Is that all?" Wolfe demanded.

"Isn't it enough, for God's sake?" Cramer roared, pounding a fist on Wolfe's desktop. "Durkin's a hothead, a damn loose cannon, but he's fired once too often. I'll see myself out," he spat, turning on his heel. "I remember the way."

I followed him down the hall and bolted the door behind him. "That wasn't very cheerful news," I told Wolfe when I got back to the office. "It must have upset Cramer, too, though. First, he didn't fling his mutilated stogie at the wastebasket—he had the decency to take it with him. Second, he didn't say boo to me on the way out, not a word, and he always throws at least one parting zinger my way."

"Among the things upon which we agree, Archie, is that Inspector Cramer is essentially an honorable man. His methods and mental processes often fall short of adequacy, although the same cannot be said of his conscientiousness. He is understandably troubled, because despite his gainsaying it, and despite this latest damning report, he is as convinced as we are that Fred is innocent. However, being a pragmatist as well, the inspector realizes that to pursue his investigation further is to in effect suggest that one church stalwart has murdered another—hardly a prudent move for a high-ranking public servant. He would be pilloried by his superiors, not to mention the treatment he would receive at the hands of some of the less responsible segments of the media." Wolfe sighed. "It falls to us alone to extricate Fred from this morass, which appears to be deepening."

"Okay, let's start extricating," I said. "What do we do next?"

Wolfe rang for more beer, then readjusted his bulk. "Visit Mrs. Meade tomorrow. Call upon your interrogatory skills to discover whatever you can about her late husband's attitudes toward his job and his coworkers. Also, return to the church and seek permission from Mr. Bay to conduct a search of Mr. Meade's office. If he balks at the request, call me."

"What am I looking for?"

He pursed his lips. "What indeed. Undoubtedly, members of the church staff—including his murderer—already have gone through Mr. Meade's papers, so whatever clues existed may have been obliterated. However, it is possible that some crumbs were overlooked by the broom. Use your intelligence, guided by experience."

I grinned. "Where have I heard that line before?"

"Wise counsel bears repetition," he said airily. "Give particular attention to Mr. Meade's Bibles. Surely there are several on his shelves. Sift through them for notations, underlinings, dog-eared pages."

"So you think *he* wrote those notes threatening Bay, huh?"

"I did not say that," Wolfe replied. "One more thing."

"Yes?"

"Attend the service at Mr. Bay's church on Sunday."

"Any particular reason? I can watch it on television. So, for that matter, can you."

Wolfe made a face. "I would like to receive the benefit of your observations and reactions," he said, drinking beer and retreating behind his book. I thought of a great comeback, but I sat on it. After all, I had gotten what I wanted—marching orders. There was nothing to be gained by alienating the field marshal.

THIRTEEN

When he gives orders, Wolfe rarely concerns himself with how they get carried out. He figures that's part of what he pays me for. So the next morning after breakfast I was in the office punching a telephone number I know by heart.

"Homicide," a gruff voice barked. I told him I wanted Cramer, who was on the line seconds later with his own heartwarming "Yeah?"

"Goodwin. I need a couple of things. The name of Mrs. Meade's employer on Wall Street, and her address on Staten Island."

"Why should I give them to you?"

"Why shouldn't you? As far as you're concerned, the case is closed, correct?"

"There's such a thing as protecting an individual's privacy, you know."

"Oh, come on, Inspector. I can find this stuff out from some other sources. I just thought it would be simpler to get it from you. For old times."

He spat a word that would have made his old

mother blush. "Old times, my flat feet. For all the grief that— Oh, hell, why am I wasting my breath? Hold on." He left the phone and was back a few seconds later with what I had asked for. I started to say thank you but found I was talking to a dial tone.

I called the Wall Street brokerage house number Cramer had given me and got told by a crisply efficient female voice that "Mrs. Meade will not be back in the office until next week. Would you like her voice mail?"

I said no to that offer. Okay, now there would be two stops on Staten Island. I went to the kitchen and told Fritz I was leaving on business and probably would be gone much of the day.

"Meaning you will miss another meal?" He shook his head in bewilderment. The brownstone was filled with people baffled by human nature.

I promised I would try to do better and walked a block to the garage where we housed the Mercedes. The sun was out and traffic was mercifully light on the tunnel-and-bridge route that took me first to Brooklyn and then to Staten Island. My trusty "Five Boroughs" folding map led me unerringly to the narrow dead-end street just off Castelton Avenue where the Meade residence, a two-story white Dutch Colonial with blue shutters, was nestled in a mini-forest of maples.

Parking beside a fire hydrant in the only available spot on the block, I used the rearview mirror to adjust my tie, a birthday gift from La Rowan. I climbed the steps to the front door and leaned on the buzzer.

"Yes?" Her face, although showing strain, was well-arranged and framed by sandy hair. She was wearing a man's-style, white button-down dress shirt and jeans. Her light blue eyes considered me without making any apparent judgment.

"Mrs. Meade?"

"That's right, I'm Sara Meade."

All the way over from Manhattan, I'd been doping out how I was going to play it. Now I said: "My name is Archie Goodwin. I am a private investigator, employed by Nero Wolfe, and you probably have no interest whatever in talking to me, let alone inviting me into your house. I understand and respect that; I will only say that Mr. Wolfe feels strongly that your husband's death was caused by someone other than the man who has been charged."

One corner of her mouth twitched, but the expression in her eyes did not change. "Do you agree with your employer, Mr. Goodwin?" she asked in a voice that was at once soft and strong.

"I do."

"I would ask for identification except that I recognize both the name and the face. Your picture has been in the newspapers before, hasn't it?"

"A couple of times, yes."

"More than a couple of times, I think. Please come in," she said, stepping aside and ushering me into a large living room with a beamed ceiling, fireplace, and American Colonial furniture. "Please sit down. Can I offer you coffee? I just poured myself some. I hope you don't mind—it's hazelnut."

I nodded and thanked her, and she was back with a steaming cup as I took a semicomfortable chair. On the end table at my elbow was a chrome-framed photograph of Sara Meade, her husband, and a light-haired boy, presumably their son, who looked to be in his teens.

"I know of course from the papers and the TV news that Fred Durkin is a colleague of yours and Mr. Wolfe's," she said, easing onto the sofa. "Does that influence your belief in his innocence?"

"I can't deny it, and I doubt that Mr. Wolfe would either, if you put the question to him. But it is precisely because Fred is a colleague, and because both of us have known him for so long, that we are convinced he is not a killer. It would be totally out of character for him."

She frowned and took a sip of coffee. "But he is a detective. And he does carry a gun."

"Yes. But I have never known him to draw it, except as a defensive gesture." I neglected to mention that I had once been the beneficiary of one such gesture.

"And he also has a temper."

I nodded, savoring the coffee. Fritz would have approved. "Yes, Mrs. Meade, he does. But, again, I probably know Fred Durkin better than anyone in the world outside of his own family and perhaps Nero Wolfe. I have seen his temper flare up on occasion, but to my knowledge, he has never—repeat, never—done violence to another individual in the heat of anger. That simply is not his style."

"Even when he's insulted?" Sara Meade set her cup carefully in its saucer and leaned forward. "I loved my husband, Mr. Goodwin—very much. But I was acutely aware of his shortcomings, as he was of mine. Despite being a minister, Roy could be extremely caustic and hard-edged. I understand he said some very harsh things to your friend in front of the Circle of Faith on . . . that night."

"I understand the same thing, and I honestly believe that what your husband said to Fred would not have impelled Fred to lash back other than verbally—which, as you know, he did."

She chewed absently on a finger. "Well, if Fred Durkin didn't fire the gun, who did? Are you suggesting it was one of the Circle of Faith? There was no one else in the tabernacle."

"Mr. Wolfe is not ruling that out, which is why I'm here. In the last few months, did your husband say anything to you that would suggest there was a rift between him and anyone at the Silver Spire? It may have been just a passing remark, something that you didn't think much about at the time."

She tapped the rim of her cup. "You've been very forthright and direct with me, Mr. Goodwin, and I appreciate that. I will be forthright in return. As I said a minute ago, Roy had a mercilessly critical side to him. He demanded a lot from the people he worked with, and he became impatient when they didn't meet his expectations. At one time or another, he complained to me about almost every one of the church staff, from Barney on down."

"What kind of complaints were they?"

"Oh, a variety," she said, gesturing with her hand. "He came down particularly hard on Roger Gillis, which always bothered me because Roger seems like such an earnest, well-meaning young man. But Roy felt—and for all I know, he was right—that Roger was really in over his head as the director of education. On more than one occasion, he publicly said that Roger wasn't a good administrator or a good organizer. Roy really wanted Roger out of the job, but he couldn't budge Barney on the subject."

"Is it true that your husband felt Bay was too easy on his staff?"

"Yes, that was a big beef of his. Roy had a phrase about Barney that he used several times: 'He tolerates mediocrity in the interest of tranquillity.' I think I'm the only one he ever said it to, though."

"It's not likely he bandied it about around the church. Your husband once saved Bay's life, didn't he?"

She nodded, suddenly looking very tired. "Yes, he rescued Barney from drowning years ago when they were ministerial students. But he never liked having the subject brought up, because he thought people would feel it was the reason Barney hired him."

"Was it?"

She shrugged. "Maybe. But I think Roy long ago proved himself."

"Did he talk much to you about other Circle of Faith members?" I asked.

"From time to time, usually out of frustration. He thought that Sam Reese was coasting in his job, that Lloyd Morgan was a functionary overly concerned with nit-picking, that Marley Wilkenson ran the music programs as a separate fiefdom and obstinately refused to answer to anyone."

"What about Mrs. Reese and Mrs. Bay?"

She laughed, which was pleasant to hear. "Lord, I sound like the town gossip, don't I? I'm glad you're not taping this."

"I'm not even taking notes."

"Good. Well, Roy never liked Carola much—he thought she was kind of on the cheap side, although he conceded that she's a fine singer. As far as Elise Bay, I can't remember him criticizing her much; he mainly complained that she shouldn't be in the Circle, that she was there only because of who she was. That bothered him about Carola, too."

"As far as you know, were any of the Circle of Faith members having financial problems?"

She wrinkled her forehead. "Roy never said anything about it that I can remember. And what you asked before—about whether there were rifts between him and any of the others. As we've talked, I've been thinking, and there *was* something Roy mentioned a few weeks back. I can't even remember how the subject came up, but—oh, I know!—I was complaining to him about someone who works for me who was falling down on the job. I said I'd warned this person twice but there hadn't been much improvement, and it looked like I was going to have to let him go. Then Roy said he had a staff problem, too, and that it would have to be dealt with."

"Can you remember his exact words?"

She closed her eyes and made a clicking noise with her tongue. "Let's see . . . I think he said something like 'I've got a situation myself. It's going to give one way or the other in the next few weeks. I've set a deadline.' "

"That was it?"

She nodded. "Yes. I asked him what he meant, what that situation was, but he didn't want to talk about it anymore. He just clammed up."

"Was that unusual behavior?"

"Not really. I know from what I've been telling you that it sounds like Roy griped about the church to me all the time, but that's really not so. I just lumped together all the things he complained about over the years. In fact, most of the time, he didn't want to talk shop at all. I unloaded a lot more about my job than he did."

"And he never brought it up again?"

"Never."

"Did he seem particularly depressed recently?"

Sara inhaled and let the air out slowly. "No, I didn't notice anything, and I think I've always been pretty sensitive to Roy's moods."

"One last thing: Have you been to the church to go through your husband's effects?"

"Oh, I did stop in to pick up a box of things, and I need to go back again. What I got was mostly mementos and pictures of me and our son. . . ." Her voice caught on the last three words. The calm facade was beginning to crumble, so I got to my feet.

"I've taken enough of your time, Mrs. Meade. I am grateful for your seeing me." I handed her my card. "If you think of anything else that might be helpful, I would appreciate a call."

"I can't honestly say that I wish you luck," she replied softly, walking me to the door and shaking my hand with a firm grip, "but I do want to have the assurance that the right person is punished, whether it's your Mr. Durkin or someone else."

"I agree completely," I said over my shoulder as I walked down the front steps, wondering how a guy as apparently disagreeable as Meade could end up with a woman like her.

FOURTEEN

Ten minutes after I left Sara Meade, I wheeled the Mercedes into the Silver Spire Tabernacle's parking lot. Except for a dozen cars huddled near the entrance, it was as empty as Shea Stadium in January. I found a spot twenty paces from the main door and sauntered into the lobby, where the redheaded receptionist was pondering *People* magazine and jawing on a stick of gum.

She looked up and unleashed both her pearly whites and her dimples. "Hi! Back again? You must like it here."

"I do. Half the fun of coming is seeing you and your smile and your outfits. That blue number is very becoming."

"Thank you," she said, blushing like a freshman on her first date. "It's my boyfriend's favorite color."

"With good reason. Say, could you call Diane and tell her that Mr. Goodwin is here and would like to see Dr. Bay?"

"My pleasure. And you didn't have to tell me your name—I remember it."

I thanked her and waited while she used the telephone. "She says to go right on back," the redhead told me as she cradled the receiver. "You know the way."

"Hello, Mr. Goodwin," Diane sang when I got to the office. The secretarial pool at the tabernacle seemed untouched by the recent murder. "Dr. Bay is in a meeting, but he knows you're here and said to wait, that he wouldn't be long."

And he wasn't. A tall, lean, bald-headed specimen that I hadn't seen before sauntered out of Bay's sanctum, nodding soberly to Diane and the other receptionist, who never seemed to look up from her typing. "You can go on in now," Diane said. Her smile wasn't as blinding as the redhead's, but it was more genuine. I smiled back.

"Hello, Mr. Goodwin," Bay said neutrally when I got within three feet of his desk. "Sorry to keep you waiting, but we weren't expecting you. I was just meeting with the chairman of our stewardship campaign. You know, the dollars-and-cents side of things." He smiled. "Everybody needs more money to operate, even us church folk."

"Your cash flow good?" I asked.

He gave his palms-up gesture. "Pledges are right on target, even slightly above. We're down a bit in our loose offering, though—that's the money, most of it currency, that we get Sundays from our one-time visitors and other nonmembers. The members almost all write checks, a lot of them monthly or quarterly.

But then, all businesses have money problems, and as I get reminded frequently, we are among other things a business."

I told Bay I wanted to spend a few minutes in Meade's office. "I'm not looking to steal anything; you can have somebody in there with me the whole time if you'd like."

"What *are* you looking for?" He smiled but narrowed his eyes.

"I won't know until I see it—if then."

Bay folded his arms across his chest. "It sounds to me a little like a fishing expedition. Up to now, we've indulged you and Mr. Wolfe, but there's a limit."

"I don't think we'll be making many requests of you after this. And I won't be here more than an hour."

"Sara—Mrs. Meade—has taken a few personal items away already, and she mentioned she'll be back for more later, when she feels up to it. Lloyd, Sam, and my secretary Diane all have been going through Roy's correspondence and other papers, mainly to make sure no church business falls between the cracks. I can't imagine what you expect to find that would help you in your . . . quest." Bay rose slowly and walked to his mullioned window, tugged a cord that opened the cream-colored draperies, and gazed out on the acres of blacktop and the Cana Chapel beyond, nestled snugly in its grove of trees. He turned back toward me as if striking a pose, then absently fingered a silver chalice on an ebony table next to the window. "Do you truly feel all this is necessary?" he asked quietly.

"It's probably just the proverbial goose chase," I

conceded. "But what have you—or the church—got to lose? Meade didn't have anything to hide, did he? And even if he had, Morgan, Reese, Diane, or his wife surely would have discovered it by now. I assume his office has been unlocked since his death."

"Of course it's been unlocked." Bay sounded offended. "All right, Mr. Goodwin," he went on, trying half heartedly to mask his irritation, "you can go ahead. I don't like this business, but I believe you to be both honest and well-intentioned." He pushed a button, and within seconds, Diane entered, wearing her ever-present smile.

"Mr. Goodwin wants to have a look at Roy's office," Bay told her. "Take him, please, and show him where everything is, and then you can leave. He'll probably be in there for an hour or so."

I followed Diane across the hall. Meade's office was slightly larger than Wilkenson's or Reese's, but not as elaborately decorated. Bookshelves covered one wall, floor to ceiling, and papers were stacked up in two neat foot-high piles on his desk.

"Mr. Morgan and Mr. Reese and I have sorted some of Mr. Meade's correspondence and his other papers, but we've got an awful lot more to go through, mainly the stuff in the filing cabinets," Diane told me. "And I don't know *what* we'll do with all the books he had. Just look at them!"

"Quite a library," I agreed. "What's in these stacks on the desk?"

"Mostly things we've gone over that don't need immediate attention, or that we don't know what to do with. It's here for Mrs. Meade to go through when she wants to. A lot of it we probably could have just

tossed, but Dr. Bay thought it best that we should save
it for her."

I agreed and said thanks, and Diane left, closing
the door behind her. My first stop was the bookcases.
Meade kept his Bibles on the lowest shelf, six of them
in all. I sat at his desk and paged through each one.
Wolfe had said to look for marginal notes and underlinings, but there weren't any. Either the guy didn't
use the Good Books much, which I doubted, or he
didn't like to mark them up. He probably was one of
those kids who always gave the teacher a birthday card
and never underlined in his school texts.

After a quick scanning of the rest of the shelves—
most of the books had "Christian" or "Christianity"
in their titles—I started on the piles on the desk.
There were brochures about upcoming Silver Spire
conferences and seminars; fliers advertising new religious books; a dozen magazines, most of them
church-oriented; some letters from ministers around
the country who apparently corresponded regularly
with Meade; and a couple of thick mail-order catalogs
filled with pictures of church furniture and para-
phernalia like candle holders and preachers' robes in
white and black and purple.

There also was a pad of white notepaper with
Meade's name and phone number printed at the top
that had some scribbled notations to call various people, none of whom was familiar to me. Tucked into
the pad was a sheet of yellow lined paper, folded once,
that also had some scribblings, in the same handwriting. I looked closer and realized they were Bible
verses, then set the sheet aside and finished rummag-

ing through the stacks without finding anything else that seemed even vaguely promising.

Diane was typing when I popped my head into the office. "Is there a copying machine I can use?" I asked. She gave me a bright-eyed nod and steered me to a sterile, fluorescent-lit, windowless room at the far end of the corridor. "This is our printing center," she said proudly, gesturing to the three personal computers and several other pieces of high technology, one of which I recognized as a mainframe.

"We're set up to do almost all of our own typesetting and printing," Diane went on, "including the bulletins for our Sunday services, the weekly newspaper that goes to every home, and the reprints of Dr. Bay's sermons that we send to TV viewers who request them. Some weeks we mail out several hundred of those, free. The only thing that has to be printed outside on a regular basis is our monthly magazine, *SpireTalk*. Have you seen a copy?"

I said I hadn't, and she promised to give me one to take home. I thanked her, and while she waited I used the copier to duplicate the page listing the Bible verses and the sheets of Meade's notepaper with the names and phone numbers on them.

"Okay, I've made copies of what I wanted. Come to Mr. Meade's office with me and watch while I put these originals back on his desk."

Diane grinned sheepishly and reddened. "Oh, now that's really not necessary." She giggled.

"It is for me. I want you to be able to tell your boss that I didn't walk off with anything. Of course, you weren't in there with me while I was going through the papers, so heaven only knows what I might have lifted and tucked away. Want to search me?"

She blushed again. "Oh, Mr. Goodwin, you are such a kidder."

"Guilty. But I insist you go into Meade's office with me. If you do, I promise to take a copy of your magazine home—and even read it." She shrugged and smiled and tagged along as I returned to the office. "Is that Meade's handwriting?" I asked, gesturing to the sheets as I put them back on the stack where I'd found them.

She squinted at each of them and nodded. "Yes, no question. Mr. Meade wasn't much for dictation. He'd give me scribbled letters to people all the time that he wanted typed, so I know his writing very well. That's it, all right. You can see that he never got an A in penmanship. I used to have a terrible time trying to read what he put down. I'm surprised those Bible verses are so neat."

"But they are his writing?"

"Yes. For once, he must have slowed down a little."

I thanked her and stopped at her desk long enough to get an issue of *SpireTalk*. It had a color photograph of the choir on the cover, with the line "The Spire's Singers Prepare for a European Tour." Maybe Wolfe would find some interesting reading inside, although I wasn't about to bet on it. In fact, I wouldn't even bet on his opening the thing.

As I was leaving the church, Roger Gillis blew into the lobby from the parking lot, his carrot-colored hair tossed by the wind. "Hello," he said stiffly, trying to flatten the orange mop with his hand. "Learned anything yet?"

"Nothing that would get the newspapers excited," I answered.

He snorted. "I'm not surprised. You're still trying to find somebody to pin Roy's murder on, aren't you? When *that's* not the mystery. Everybody knows who did it, and the police have already got him. The real question is, who wrote the notes to Barney? But you don't even care about them—you just want to find some way to get your pal off. And you also don't care who gets hurt in the process. Roy was right, rest his soul: You guys really *are* sleazy."

Having thus put me in my place, Gillis strutted off in the general direction of his office, no doubt thinking I would lick my wounds and slink out. I didn't slink, though, I strode, after first smiling at the redheaded receptionist, who gave her dimples another workout by smiling back.

The drive to Manhattan was a little slower than the morning trip, and by the time I got the car tucked in at the garage and climbed the front steps of the brownstone, it was ten after four, which of course meant Wolfe was playing in the plant rooms. I went to the kitchen, where Fritz worked on dinner. He gave me a sorrowful look and reported that there were no lunch leftovers. "He ate all of the veal, Archie. I am sorry."

"Hey, don't be. Having feasted on your cutlets for years, I can't blame him. I'll make myself a sandwich."

Fritz started to protest, but I stilled him with an

upraised palm, built myself a ham-on-rye, poured a glass of milk, and went to my desk in the office. As I ate, I looked at the photocopies of Meade's writing. The names and phone numbers I set aside, figuring the Bible verses were more promising, although I didn't know the hows and whys.

The phone rang—it was Lon Cohen. "Maybe you remember me. The guy you call when you need information, but the guy you forget when *he* needs information."

"Oh yeah, now I remember, the guy who helps to lighten my wallet at the gaming table every Thursday night."

He made a sound that was a cross between a growl and a chuckle. "What's going on with Durkin? He won't come to the phone when I call—never mind that I've known him for years. And Parker doesn't return my calls, but then, that's a lawyer for you. Come across, Archie, give me something for tomorrow's home edition. This story's gone into the dumpster for days now."

"Sorry, but I've got nothing to give. I'm as anxious as you are—hell, *more* anxious—to have something happen."

"What's Wolfe think?"

"Damned if I know. He rarely unburdens himself to me. Listen, you know that if and when something pops around here, you'll be the first one I call."

"Yeah. Can I get that in writing?"

"My word—spoken—is my bond," I told him, getting a word in reply before the line went dead. I turned back to the sheet of paper in my hand.

I'm the first to admit my ignorance of the Bible,

but when I was in confirmation class more years ago than you'll get me to own up to, I memorized all the books of both the Old and New Testaments, and I got a red-and-gold pin for being the first one to do it. Never mind that I didn't bother to learn what was in those books, beyond a few "begats" and "thou shalt nots."

So much for my biblical training. I stared at Meade's notations and wondered what, if anything, Wolfe would make of them. There were seven verses, neatly scripted and spaced out about three lines apart on the yellow sheet:

1 Tim 6:10
Job 5:16
Acts 17:28
Matt 2:12
Psalm 86:13
Eccles 5:17
Rom 13:14

I briefly contemplated pulling one of Wolfe's Bibles off the shelf and trying to make something out of all this, but I finished my sandwich instead, then started in on updating the orchid-germination records. I know how to use the old noodle, but I also know my limitations. On our team, Wolfe is the brains, and I'm the legs and the eyes and the sweat, when sweat is called for, which is most of the time. By and large, that division of authority works pretty well, and I wasn't about to mess with it.

FIFTEEN

I was still at the computer when I heard the groaning of the elevator at six. Wolfe entered the office, slipped an orchid into the vase on his desk, got settled, and rang for beer. "The veal cutlets were superb," he announced.

"So was my ham sandwich—take it from the man who made it. I put some reading material on the blotter. You want to go over it first, or should I report?"

He raised his eyebrows. "These verses?"

"The best I could do. Meade apparently wasn't big on marking up his Bibles. But I found that list on his desk, along with the names and phone numbers."

Wolfe pulled in a bushel of air. "Report," he said, pouring beer into a glass from one of two bottles Fritz had just brought in. I gave him my usual playback, which took just over twenty minutes. He sat with his eyes closed, opening them occasionally to locate his glass and lift it to his lips. When I finished, he studied the sheet with the verses. "Get Mr. Bay," he said.

"It's after six. He's probably gone home."

"You are resourceful, as you remind me daily."

"Yes, sir." I punched the church's number and got a recorded woman's voice informing me that the office hours were nine to five daily and reciting the times of the Sunday services. It ended by giving a number that could be called in case of emergency. I decided this was not an emergency and called directory assistance for Bay's home number. They had it, which was a mild surprise. Wolfe already was on the line when the man himself answered.

"Mr. Bay? Nero Wolfe. I need information."

"Can't it wait till tomorrow?" he asked plaintively. "My wife and I are just sitting down to dinner."

"This will take but a moment. At the time of his death, was Mr. Meade in the process of preparing a sermon?"

"No . . . not that I know of. I'm not taking another vacation until November. Roy probably would have been in the pulpit at least one of the weeks I was to be gone, but we hadn't discussed it yet."

"Might he have been scheduled to preach elsewhere?"

"Unlikely," Bay replied. "Roy didn't give guest sermons very often, although he certainly was free to do so. And when he did, I usually knew about it, because he almost always asked my advice on content and organization."

"The reason for my questions is that Mr. Goodwin discovered a listing of Bible passages on Mr. Meade's desk today," Wolfe said. "Seven of them. The first is I Timothy 6:10."

"The most misquoted verse of all," Bay said.

"Inarguably."

"As I'm sure you know, in most modern trans-lations it reads something like 'the love of money is the root of all kinds of evil.' But the words 'the love of' seem to get dropped when the passage is cited—at least by lay people."

"Can you suggest any reason Mr. Meade might have set down these passages?" Wolfe read the other six for Bay.

"No," the minister answered. "Diane told me that Mr. Goodwin had made a photocopy of some material from Roy's office, and I was going to take a look at the originals tomorrow. I will not claim to be an expert on every verse in the Bible, Mr. Wolfe, but from what I do know, those you mentioned just now don't seem to follow a particular pattern. Roy probably was using them in his own personal devotions, for whatever spe-cific reasons he had. That's not at all unusual. I often make note of certain verses myself when I'm reading the Bible. They help me to focus both my thoughts and my prayers."

Wolfe thanked Bay and cradled the receiver, studying the verses again. He glared at his empty glass before refilling it, then walked to the bookshelves and pulled a Bible out, carrying it back to the desk. He thumbed through it, stopping occasionally to make a notation on a sheet of bond I had supplied at his request.

"Finding anything?" I asked sociably after several minutes. I got a grunt in response. He repeated the process with a second Bible from the shelf and a third, and judging by the expression on his face, he had discovered no more in them than he had in the first.

He still had all three of the books open on the desk when Fritz announced dinner.

Wolfe seemed like his usual self at the table, polishing off three helpings of the salmon mousse with dill sauce—his own recipe—and launching into a monologue on why the country consistently elects Republican Presidents and Democratic Congresses. The way he laid it out, it made perfect sense to me.

When we were back in the office after dinner, I started to get worried. First off, Wolfe didn't ring for beer after he'd finished his coffee. He just sat for five minutes with his hands on the arms of the chair and his eyes shut, then closed the Bibles, returned them to the shelves, and announced he was going to bed. It was nine o'clock, and he never turns in much before midnight. It had all the earmarks of that most dreaded of Wolfe's maladies—a relapse.

I have never figured out what brings on the relapses, but he's been having them all the years I've been on the payroll. He doesn't get one on every case—not even close. And he doesn't necessarily fall into them on the most difficult cases. But when one comes, nothing short of a five-alarm fire in his bedroom will blast him out of it. I've seen these things last anywhere from one day to two weeks, and in the extreme, I've known him to quit altogether. That happened in the Farnstrom Jewelry swindle, which never did get solved, and we had to give back a retainer that would have kept Wolfe in beer, books, and beluga caviar for months, never mind that he doesn't eat caviar.

I went to bed hoping the evening's performance

had been a false alarm, but it didn't take me long the next morning to learn otherwise. "He is not himself, Archie," Fritz said glumly when I came down to the kitchen for breakfast. "I can tell."

"All right, how can you tell?" If I sounded irritated, it was because I didn't want to believe him.

"He had that look he gets when he . . ."

"When he *what*?" I snapped.

I instantly regretted my tone, because Fritz looked like he'd just been slapped. He clenched his fists in frustration. "When he . . . when he gives up. You know how he is then, you have seen it, too. That's how he looked when I took his breakfast up to him."

"Relapse." There, I said the word, and we nodded to each other.

"Okay, we've been through this drill before," I told him. "There's not a hell of a lot we can do when he's like this, and we both know it. He usually goes one of two ways—either he stays in his room like a hermit, or he parks himself here in the kitchen and tells you how to do your work, right down to the sage and the chives and God knows, even the paprika or whatever. Remember the time he camped in the kitchen and ate half a sheep in two days? Cooked God knows how many different ways? For your sake, I hope he does the hermit bit."

"Twenty different ways. Archie, I don't want him to do either thing. I just want him to go to work," Fritz said, cupping his hands and looking at the ceiling.

"Me too. We'll just have to hope this is one of the shorter spells."

Wolfe apparently went up to play with the orchids directly from his bedroom at nine as usual, because I heard the drone of the elevator. That part of his schedule at least remained intact. At eleven, as I sat in the office typing some correspondence he had dictated the day before, the elevator whirred again, but it never got to the first floor—a bad sign. Ten minutes later, Fritz was in the office looking even more woebegone than earlier. "He called me on the kitchen phone and said he wants his lunch brought up to him in his room. That is bad . . . very, very bad."

"The good news is that he's not hounding you in the kitchen. The bad news is, he's definitely, positively in a relapse. And as usual in one of these things, the schedule's out the window. Man your battle stations and be prepared for anything."

Fritz didn't appreciate the attempt at humor, and I wasn't amused by it myself. As Wolfe's relapses go, this ended up being medium-long—about one hundred eighteen hours if you count it as beginning after dinner Wednesday. He stayed in his room all of Thursday, Friday, Saturday, and Sunday, except for his twice-daily trips to commune with the orchids.

When these things occur, I make it a point not to let them alter my personal life. As I do once a week, I played poker that night at Saul Panzer's. I was picked almost clean for most of the evening, but I won the last three pots—one of them on a bluff—and walked away only fifteen bucks in the hole, which was a moral victory, because I had been down more than fifty. Friday I was Lily Rowan's escort at a fancy dinner party for twelve in a palatial duplex on Sutton Place. The food was almost as good as Fritz's, and I even knew which forks to use with what courses. And Saturday, Saul and I went to a Rangers-Washington playoff game at the Garden, which the Rangers won in three overtimes. One of the Sunday papers said it was "the most thrilling game in hockey history." Maybe.

For the next several days, the only event related to the case, other than two "what-have-you-got-for-me?" calls from Lon Cohen, was when Nathaniel Parker phoned on Friday. "How's Wolfe coming with this thing?" he asked smoothly.

"Working on it," I lied.

"Well, Durkin's a basket case wondering what kind of progress is being made. He doesn't want to call you guys, for fear Wolfe will get angry with him. And he's not answering his phone, because the press has been all over him the last few days. They've staked out his place in Queens, and when his wife went out to pick the morning paper off the front stoop yesterday, a TV crew rushed the house and tried to interview her. She slammed the door in their faces."

"Good for Fanny. I always did like her style. Next time Fred calls, tell him things are moving along."

Parker snorted. "Your tone doesn't exactly instill confidence."

"Well, you know Wolfe. He plays it pretty close to his oversized vest."

"We haven't got forever," Parker cautioned before signing off. That's a lawyer for you, always full of cheering observations.

Fritz gave me periodic reports on Wolfe's condition, given that he took a meal tray up to his room three times a day. "His appetite is excellent, Archie. I think that's a good sign, don't you?" he told me Friday afternoon.

"Nuts to his appetite. I'm going up." I took the steps two at a time to the second floor and rapped on his door. "It's me," I said. "We need to talk."

He said something like "Come in," and I opened the door. He was propped up in bed wearing his yellow pajamas and reading. For some reason, he always seems larger when he's in bed, maybe because of all that yellow—not only his pajamas, but the sheets and coverlet as well. He gave me a questioning scowl.

"Pardon the interruption, but are you planning to return to work sometime soon? Say, before Fred Durkin is shipped off to Attica to spend the rest of his days making license plates, or whatever it is they do at those places now?"

"I just read something very interesting, Archie," the resident genius said in a chatty tone, gesturing to the book he was holding. "Did you know that the first English factory to use steam power was that of Josiah Wedgwood, the maker of china?"

"I have to admit that comes as a surprise, and I'm certainly glad to see that you're enjoying your reading. Just as a matter of curiosity, will you be back in the office in the near future, or should I have it redecorated as a shrine to your past glories? We could probably help with the upkeep of the brownstone by charging admission. It may turn out to be our only income."

He closed his eyes. "Sarcasm has never been among your strengths, Archie. You would do well to excise it from your repertoire."

"Yes, sir. My question stands."

"At the moment, I am immersed in this volume. I would like to complete it in peace. Good day."

I thought about going to the office, getting my Marley, and finishing him off, but that wouldn't help Fred any. Instead, I smiled and walked out, closing the door quietly behind me and giving myself an A+ in restraint.

SIXTEEN

On Sundays, the brownstone's normal schedule sails out the window. Fritz frequently takes the day off, and if Wolfe visits the plant rooms, it's usually for just a short time. More often than not, he whiles away the hours in the office with the Sunday papers or a book, occasionally wandering out to the kitchen to whip up some sustenance for himself.

On this Sunday, the fourth full day of the relapse, Wolfe kept to his room and Fritz stayed around because "He may need me, Archie." I suggested to Fritz that he disappear for a few hours and let his employer fend for himself, but that isn't his style. And damned if he didn't wait on the lord and master, bustling up to his bedroom first with a breakfast tray, then with the *Times*.

I read both the *Times* and the *Gazette* at my desk after eating in the kitchen. No mention was made of Meade's murder—there hadn't been anything about it in either paper since early in the week. In New York, yesterday's headline is today's ancient history. I put-tered in the office for a while, straightening things that didn't need straightening. Finally I got so disgusted with Fritz's kowtowing to Wolfe—by nine-thirty, he had made four trips to the second floor—that I left for the Silver Spire before I had planned to. Anything to get out of Chez Relapse.

At that, I arrived at the church none too early, as I discovered when I wheeled the Mercedes into the big parking lot at ten-twenty-two. The blacktop already was well over half filled with cars ranging from Lincolns and BMWs to subcompacts, and a platoon of earnest, well-scrubbed young men in dark slacks and white, open-collared shirts deftly motioned drivers into spaces, neatly filling one row at a time.

I fell into step with dozens of others zeroing in on the tabernacle doors; except that most of us were dressed in going-to-church clothes, we could as easily have been surging toward the gates of the Meadowlands to see the Giants knock heads with the Redskins—although there were no bratwurst-scented tailgate parties in the tabernacle lot.

Inside the gold-and-chrome lobby, I took stock of my fellow worshipers: The majority were in their twenties and thirties, almost all of them white. My instant survey told me slightly more than half were couples, and that the overall man-woman makeup of the crowd was too close to call.

I sauntered to a counter along one wall that was manned by two grandmotherly types and stocked with pamphlets and books, including Bay's *Inspiration Theology*, on sale for six-ninety-five in paperback and eleven-ninety-five in hardcover. I selected instead a free brochure headlined "What the Silver Spire Ministry Can Mean in Your Life" and moved toward the auditorium. Like the parking lot, it already was well-filled, and organ music wafted over the crowd.

A perky young woman with long red hair, a handful of programs, and a badge identifying her as "Jennie Amundsen—Usher" greeted me. She wore one of those little spire-shaped lapel pins just above the badge on her light blue dress. "Hi, do you worship with us regularly?" she asked as she slipped me a program.

"No, this is my first visit; I'm from out of town," I improvised cleverly.

"Well, we're really happy to have you with us today, Mr. . . ."

"Goodman." I was on a roll with my new identity.

"How far down would you like to sit, Mr. Good-man?" Her smile was dazzling.

I said about halfway would be fine, and she led me to a single open seat on the aisle next to a couple who looked to be about ten years out of high school. As I eased into the cushioned theater-type seat, they both pivoted my way with grins as big as Jennie Amundsen's. "Hi, I'm Cal Warren," said the full-faced, prematurely balding male half of the pair, who occupied the seat adjoining mine. He thrust a thick paw at me, vigorously shaking hands. "This is my wife, Darlene." She nodded a head of short blond hair, and her blue eyes danced. She probably didn't push the pointer on her bathroom scale over the one hundred mark, while her husband easily doubled that figure.

"You a member here?" Cal asked in a breezy tone.

"No, I'm in from out of town on business."

"That's what usually happens to us." He laughed

with satisfaction. "You see, Darlene and me—we've been members for five years now—every Sunday we sit here so there's just the one seat between us and the aisle, you know? That way, we almost always meet a first-timer, somebody like yourself who's giving us a try here at the Spire. Darlene and me, we just love to meet new people. Where are you from, Mr. . . . ?"

"Goodman. Alan Goodman. Chillicothe, Ohio."

"Ohio. A doggone nice place, from what I've seen of it so far. I get over to Cincy once or twice a year in my work. Darlene went with me once. You liked it, too, didn't you, honey?"

She nodded and made her eyes dance again. "How did you find out about the Silver Spire, Mr. Goodman?" she asked. "Have you seen our service on television?"

I told her I had a friend back home who recommended it, and she looked as if she was ready to ask another question when the lighting intensified, probably for the TV cameras, and a trumpet fanfare blasted from somewhere behind us, halting the murmurs throughout the big auditorium, where every seat now was taken. I turned and saw that the trumpeting came from three men in maroon blazers standing in one corner of the balcony. They stopped as abruptly as they had begun, and on their note, Barnabas Bay strode purposefully across the stage to the lectern that I knew—thanks to Nella Reid's tour—had only seconds before been hydraulically raised from out of the floor. Bay was wearing a light gray suit, a blue patterned tie, and the hint of a smile.

"Good morning, brothers and sisters," he intoned, spreading his arms wide, palms up. "Welcome again to our Hour of Glory. And to start us off right, the Spire Choir, directed of course by our own Marley Wilkenson, reminds us of 'What a Friend We Have in Jesus.' "

With that, the choir, some sixty strong on risers at stage left and resplendent in silver-and-crimson robes, poured out one of the hymns I grew up on back home. Wilkenson was plenty theatrical in his directing, waving his arms more than a midtown traffic cop during the evening rush hour. And on the last verse, he pivoted smartly toward the audience and urged us all to stand and sing, which we did—following words projected on a screen above the choir. I spotted Carola in the center of the first row of singers—she's hard to miss—but I'm sure she didn't notice me, just another face in the crowd.

After the hymn, Wilkenson wiped his brow with a handkerchief and bowed. "You're all in marvelous voice this fine morning," he boomed into his lapel mike. "Now I want you to welcome a truly gifted young musician to our stage. She's only nine, but she plays the violin like a Stern or a Perlman." He introduced a taffy-haired little girl in a pink dress and petticoats who knew how to use her violin, all right. For those who were sitting more than a block from the stage, and there seemed to be plenty of them, her televised, twelve-foot image loomed on yet another screen, which had been noiselessly lowered from a groove in the ceiling. Lily probably could have identified the piece she played; whatever it was, it sounded good.

After she finished and bowed to the applause, Bay came back on stage, put an arm around her shoulders, and said, "Isn't she wonderful, folks? What a gift. Her parents, Tom and Marie, are right down front here; they've been members of our Spire family for—what?—twelve years, isn't it?" He looked toward the couple, who sat in the second row and nodded. "And, honey, you've been coming to Sunday school here for how long?" Bay bent down and thrust his microphone at the girl.

"Seven years," the small voice responded.

"Seven years—isn't that great?" he beamed. "Let's give her another Spire-style round of applause." We all did, and the girl left the stage while Bay resumed his place at the lectern, his expression now somber. He looked out over the crowd and said nothing for fully fifteen seconds. He then squared his shoulders.

"Brothers and sisters in Christ, I stand before you this morning heavy with sadness, weighted with grief. As most of you here in the tabernacle, and"—he stretched an arm dramatically—"many, many of you watching us from across the country and around the globe know, our beloved brother and friend at the Silver Spire, Roy Meade, has gone to take a place with his Father above. We cry out at the injustice of Roy's sudden death, his violent death, his inexplicable death. We—or at least I—ask Almighty God why, oh why, have you allowed such a thing to happen to one of your good and faithful servants?" Bay's shoulders sagged, and he paused once more, letting his eyes move over the hushed audience.

"There is an answer to this question, my friends," the preacher said in a rising voice. "And, of course, it is here." He held a Bible aloft and let it fall open on his palm. "Please take your own Bibles and come with me now to Paul's letter to the Romans, chapter eight. I am reading as usual from the New International Version."

The sound of turning pages filled the hall. Cal and Darlene Warren each opened their Bibles, and Cal held his so I could read along. "Starting with verse thirty-five: 'Who can separate us from the love of Christ? Shall trouble or hardship or persecution or famine or nakedness or danger or sword? As it is written: For your sake we face death all day long; we are considered as sheep to be slaughtered. No, in all these things we are more than conquerors through him who loved us. For I am convinced that neither death nor life, neither angels nor demons, neither the present nor the future, nor any powers, nor height nor depth, nor anything else in all creation, will be able to separate us from the love of God that is in Christ Jesus our Lord.'"

Bay closed the Bible loudly and leaned forward, resting his elbows on the lectern. "Brothers and sisters," he said gravely, spacing his words for effect, "God has a plan for each one of us, and whatever that plan may be, nothing—repeat, nothing—can separate us from His love through Jesus Christ. You may be assured that God has a role for our beloved friend and colleague Roy, and it is not given to us to comprehend that role; it is all part of our Lord's grand plan."

Bay then launched into a sermon on death and salvation, and although much of it I either didn't agree with or didn't understand, I had to concede that the guy was one high-octane speaker. He talked for twenty-five minutes, again using his southern-tinged voice like a musical instrument—now loud, now soft, almost a whisper—and there weren't more than a couple of coughs the entire time from the three thousand plus in the audience.

After the sermon, we sang a hymn, the collection got taken—I put a finif in the offering pouch to be sociable—and we sang another hymn. Wilkenson's choir got to perform once more, too, and in between all this, Bay led us in prayer. We closed with a singing version of the Lord's Prayer, and as I rose to leave, Cal Warren stopped me. "Pardon me, Mr. Goodman," he said with a wide smile, "but have you got a card?"

"I . . . left mine at the hotel. Forgetful of me, sorry."

"Well, how's about writing your name and address down for me? I'd be happy to send you some material on the Spire." I told him I'd already taken a brochure, which I proudly produced from my breast pocket, but the boy was insistent. I tore a sheet of blank paper from my pocket secretary and wrote "Alan Goodman, Route 1, Chillicothe, Ohio" on it, feeling slightly guilty.

"How 'bout the zip code?" he asked.

"Oh, yeah, sorry." I took the paper back and scribbled the five numbers I had long ago memorized from sending cards and letters west. Never mind that anything Cal mailed would either be returned or end up in the Chillicothe Post Office's dead-letter department. We shook hands, and Darlene Warren smiled with her dancing eyes, saying she hoped I'd come back. I answered that I would try, not wanting to total up the number of fibs I had told in the last hour. And in a church, no less.

The cars moved out of the huge parking lot remarkably well, probably because of all those young men in the white shirts plus several of New York's Finest who were waving traffic through intersections in a radius of several blocks around the tabernacle. A half-hour after I turned the key in the ignition, I had the Mercedes back in the garage on Tenth Avenue.

My watch told me it was twelve-fifty-six. I contemplated going back to the brownstone, but the thought of being under the same roof as Mr. Relapse was more than I could handle at the moment, so I went for a walk.

New York takes plenty of knocks both from within and without, most of them well-deserved. The city, at least Manhattan, is overpriced, overcrowded, and dirty, and everything from bridges to subways seems to be wearing out and falling apart faster than the funds can be found to patch them up. To say nothing of miseries like random violence, drugs, and homelessness. But despite its appalling and maybe insurmountable problems, the place still possesses a fascination for me, although I can't always tell you why. That early afternoon, with spring showing its best, I felt that old pull once again.

Part of it had to be the weather: sunny, seventy, and slightly breezy. I ambled east to an almost traffic-free Fifth Avenue and turned north, eventually finding myself at Rockefeller Center, where I looked down into the sunken plaza. Brunch was being served at umbrella-sheltered tables on the very spot where ice skaters—Lily Rowan and I among them—had cavorted only two months earlier. I briefly considered hiking another half-mile or so to Lily's penthouse, but I nixed the idea faster than you can say Renoir, one of whose paintings hangs on her living-room wall. Lily loves to sleep late—very late—on Sundays, and far be it from me to disturb other people's routines. Besides, in my present state, I hardly qualified as good company.

I headed back south, this time taking Park Avenue for variety and slipping a sawbuck into the paw of a grizzled panhandler at Forty-eighth who gave me a toothless smile and a hoarse "God bless you, sir." I almost asked if he had ever been to one of Bay's homeless shelters.

Picking up my pace, I chewed over the situation one more time. Fred sat at home in Queens sweating and moping, not that I blamed him. Wolfe also sat at home, with his brain on strike—and I *did* blame him. I tried him and found him guilty of terminal laziness in the first degree. One of six people—seven, counting Bay—had to have been Meade's killer. But what was the motive? True, the guy hadn't exactly been Mr. Popularity at the church, but if healthy dislike for a fellow employee were stimulus enough for murder, most of the New York work force would wind up either in jail or pushing up posies.

I was still on the fence about Carola Reese. I had told Wolfe I'd give slightly more than even money that she had something going on the side with Wilkenson, and I wasn't ready to change my mind. Even if she and Wilkenson were playing games, though, what did Meade have to gain from harassing her? And if he blew the whistle on them, what was in it for him, other than seeing them both tossed out of the Circle of Faith and maybe out of the church as well? Was fear of being exposed great enough to spur one of them to commit murder? And was this the "situation" that Meade had mentioned to his wife? And what about the fact that Meade had known of Carola's child? How much did she fear that would get out? Enough to silence him?

Then there were Gillis and Reese. Meade hadn't endeared himself to either of them with his carping about their job performance, and he apparently held a low opinion of Morgan as well. Was one of them so terrified of losing his job that he got rid of his primary critic? I gave each of those possibilities long odds—particularly Morgan.

And I still couldn't generate much enthusiasm for either of the Bays as the culprit. Religion and I have barely a nodding acquaintance, but nonetheless, the thought of the head man at a church—any church—being a murderer struck me as implausible to the point of absurdity. And although I knew now that Elise Bay had a deep-seated dislike for Meade, I couldn't conceive of a circumstance in which she would feel compelled to kill him. Wolfe might scoff at that conclusion, claiming as he has before that beauty often blinds me to reality. Maybe he's right, but unless Meade was doing something to threaten Bay's life or his ministry, Elise was clean.

So there I was, with a boss who refused to work, a friend who was one quick trial away from prison, and a bunch of religious types, none of whom liked Meade much, but none of whom seemed to have a strong motive for dispatching him. And now we had two sets of Bible verses—the ones threatening Bay and the ones I found on Meade's desk. What, if anything, was the connection between them?

As I walked, I kept asking myself questions, but I wasn't getting any answers, and by the time I climbed the steps to the brownstone, I was good and mad.

"Is he still up in his room pouting?" I snapped at Fritz, who was sitting in the kitchen reading pieces of the Sunday paper. He took off his half-glasses and nodded. "But, Archie, he *did* come down to the office for a while. It was most unusual—he turned on the television set."

"Interesting. What did he watch?"

"I don't know. I took coffee to him just as he turned it on, and he had me shut the door when I left. It was closed the whole time he was there. Then he went back to his room, where he has been ever since."

"When was this?"

"He came down about eleven and was in the office for at least an hour. I am worried about him, Archie. He is behaving very strangely."

"I wouldn't fret. You know I'm not much for giving orders—I usually take them. This is a special case, though. Am I correct in assuming that you want to see Mr. Wolfe snap out of this funk?"

"Of course, Archie."

"Okay, take off. It's a beautiful day, absolutely gorgeous. The air will do you good. I promise to maintain things here."

Fritz set his glasses on the butcher's block and frowned. "Archie, if I leave, are you going to pick a fight with him?"

"Me? Not a chance—my middle name is Peaceful.

Now give yourself a break. See a movie. Eat a pizza. Smile at a pretty woman. It's spring, and the Mets are in first place."

Fritz shrugged and took off his apron, but he was still frowning and shaking his head as he headed for his basement apartment. He stopped in the doorway and turned back. "He will be ringing for beer again soon."

"I know where to find it," I answered, reaching for the *Times* "Week in Review" section he had left on the butcher's block. I had read about a terrorist attack in the Occupied West Bank, a banking scandal in Arizona, and student riots in Paris when the buzzer from Wolfe's bedroom sounded twice—his signal for beer. I got two chilled bottles of Remmers from the refrigerator, put them on the circular brass tray Fritz uses, and marched up the stairs, rapping twice on Wolfe's door and opening it.

He was dressed in a brown suit, yellow shirt, and brown-and-gold silk tie and was parked at the small table near the window working the *Times* Sunday Magazine's crossword puzzle. He scowled. "Where is Fritz?"

"I told him to enjoy the rest of the day," I said lightly, taking the bottles from the tray and placing them in front of him. "He gets Sundays off, remember?"

"Thank you, Mr. Goodwin." His voice had all the warmth of a glacier.

"My pleasure. Did you enjoy watching the services from the Silver Spire?"

If the question surprised Wolfe, he didn't show it. He tilted his head and scowled. "That was not a service, it was a performance. And every ten minutes, the ritual was interrupted and Mr. Bay appeared on the screen making a tasteless appeal for money. If I had dialed a telephone number, I would have received a Bible with a hand-tooled cover that was autographed by Mr. Bay. Preposterous."

"Yeah, I agree. Those of us in the church missed that particular bit of marketing. Could you spot me in the crowd?"

"I wasn't searching for you."

"Too bad. Well, now that you've had a chance to see Bay and Company in action on the tube, what's the plan?"

Wolfe treated me to a world-class growl. "*My* plan is to continue with what I was doing when you interrupted me," he snorted.

"All right," I shot back, "I'll leave you to your precious puzzle. But before I go, you should know it is my intention to turn in my resignation to you first thing tomorrow morning."

"Twaddle."

"No, sir, not twaddle. You see, I have this good friend—actually, he saved my life once, and I know he'd do it again, given the opportunity. He's in a terrible jam now, accused of a crime that I know he did not commit. Anyway, nobody else seems interested in helping him, and as long as I'm working here, my duties prevent me from devoting full time to proving him innocent. I really have no choice." I shrugged. "I am honor bound to do this. Because my weeks as your employee always end on Sundays, I will finish out the day. And I'll even be here tomorrow morning at eleven—in the office—to go over with you the status of the orchid-germination records, the correspondence, and your other files. And I'll show you where I keep the disks for the personal computer. If you do not choose to come down at eleven, I will leave a detailed memo on your desk."

Wolfe glowered at me. "I know you're probably angry," I went on, "and I don't blame you. After all these years, you have every right to expect at least two weeks' notice from me, maybe even a month. Well, I can't give you that—at least not now. My friend's predicament is too grave. However, in lieu of notice, I will pay for two weeks' salary for a first-rate temporary secretary. And while that person is here working, you can be interviewing my replacement. Fair enough?"

He glowered again, saying nothing. I nodded, did a snappy about-face, and left the room.

I have wondered since what would have happened if Wolfe had not come down to the office that Monday morning. As my watch hands inched toward the hour, I tried to busy myself with what paperwork there was. And yes, I was prepared to write that memo.

At eleven, I heard the elevator start. I kept working as it descended and then stopped. I heard the footsteps in the hall and then in the office. "Good morning, Archie, did you sleep well?" Wolfe asked as he skirted his desk and settled in behind it.

"Like a baby," I responded, not looking up.

"Good. As Swinburne wrote, 'Sleep, and be glad while the world endures,' " he said as he began going through the mail I had placed on his blotter. At least I assumed that's what he was doing, because I refused

to look up from typing my letter of resignation, although at one point I heard him leave his chair and
walk to the bookshelves, then return. When I had
finished the letter, I swiveled and saw that he was
leaning over an open Bible reading, and three others
were stacked on his left.

I kept typing, then shuffling papers, and glancing
at Wolfe as he turned pages in first one Bible and then
another, and another. This went on for a half-hour.
I was running out of ways to look occupied when he
exhaled loudly, leaning back in his chair, closing his
eyes. One of two things had happened: He had given
up, or he found something. I froze and watched him.
For ten minutes, he was as still as I was. Anyone peering in the window would have written both of us off
as either dead or catatonic.

Then it happened. At first, there was just a twitch
on his upper lip, but I knew what was coming. He
gripped the chair arms tightly with both hands, and
his lips began pushing out and in, out and in. Fritz,
probably wondering why Wolfe hadn't rung for beer
by this time, appeared in the doorway, and I silenced
him with an index finger to my mouth.

Fritz returned to the kitchen and Wolfe's lip exercise continued for nineteen minutes, which is short-
to-average for these things, and I should know; I've
timed them for years. When he opened his eyes, he
looked at me and growled. "Inexcusable," he muttered.

"What is?"

"My utter lack of perspicacity. I should be publicly
flayed."

"I'll try to arrange it," I said, but got no reaction.

He was hunched over one of the Bibles again, writing rapidly with a pen on a sheet of bond. When he finished, he pushed back and rang for beer.

"Well?" I asked. The folds in his cheeks deepened, which means he's smiling. He moved the sheet across his desk toward me. I could read his precise handwriting—that was easy—but I had no idea what I was supposed to be getting from it. He had copied the seven verses Meade had listed:

I Tim. 6:10
For the love of money is the root of all kinds of evil. Some people, eager for money, have wandered from the faith and pierced themselves with many griefs.

Job 5:16
So the poor have hope, and injustice shuts its mouth.

Acts 17:28
For in him we live and move and have our being. As some of your poets have said, "We are his offspring."

Matt. 2:12
And having been warned in a dream not to go back to Herod, they returned to their country by another route.

Psalms 86:13
For great is your love toward me; you have delivered me from the depths of the grave.

<u>Eccles. 5:17</u>
All his days he eats in darkness, with great frustration, affliction and anger.

<u>Romans 13:14</u>
Rather, clothe yourselves with the Lord Jesus Christ, and do not think about how to gratify the desires of the sinful nature.

I read through the verses twice and then looked at Wolfe, who was leaning back with his eyes closed and his hands interlaced over his center mound. "Okay, you're gloating, and the reason—or at least part of it—is that I don't have the faintest damn idea what to make of all this."

He opened his eyes and nodded thanks to Fritz, who had just brought in beer and a glass. "Gloating? Hardly," he intoned, pouring beer and watching the foam settle. "Given my utter lack of inspiration, I am in no position to gloat to you, or to anyone else." He then laid it all out for me, chapter and verse, so to speak. The way he explained it made perfect sense, although I never would have doped the thing out myself.

"Now what?" I asked.

He drained his glass and dabbed his lips with a handkerchief. "Type those verses into your computer just as I have written them—they will easily fit on a single sheet. Then print out a dozen copies. We will need them tonight."

"Which means I've got to call the Spire bunch and try to cajole them all into coming here."

Wolfe came forward in his chair. "Is this not the night the Circle of Faith meets in the church?"

"That's right—Mondays, at seven-thirty."

"Very well. We will become a nondocketed item on their agenda."

It took several seconds for what he said to sink in. The mountain was going to Mohammed.

SEVENTEEN

After recovering from the shock of Wolfe's decision, I went to the kitchen with the news that we would be leaving the brownstone about a half-hour before we normally sit down to dinner. Fritz looked at me as if I'd just salted his cassoulet castelnaudry without first tasting it.

"But—to go without eating, Archie," he pleaded. "That is bad for him . . . it is terrible!"

"Oh, come on. As good as your shrimp bordelaise is, it'll do him good to bypass a few calories now and again. It's not as if he's been wasting away. Besides, you're the one who likes to see him working." I avoided mentioning that there would be no fee on this escapade; if I had, Fritz's jaw, already sagging, would have dropped all the way to the parquet floor. As I left the kitchen, he was staring at the stove, shaking his head, and muttering something in French—probably a curse on me and all that I hold dear. And I was cursing myself for missing the shrimp, to say nothing of dessert—Fritz's incomparable pistachio soufflé.

The rest of the day seemed like a week. After lunch, which was curried beef roll, I balanced the checkbook and entered the Bible verses into the PC, per Wolfe's instructions. I then printed out twelve copies and slipped them into a manila envelope. All the while, he sat at his desk reading and drinking beer—until it was time to go up and dally with the orchids, that is.

Instead of coming down to the office at six from the plant rooms, as is his usual routine, Wolfe went to his bedroom, presumably to change for the trek to Staten Island. At six-fifty, he still hadn't descended, so I told Fritz I was leaving and walked to the garage on Tenth Avenue. I got the Mercedes and pulled it around in front of the brownstone. Wolfe was standing on the stoop, clad in his dark cashmere overcoat and homburg despite the warm weather and armed with his redthorn walking stick.

He glowered at the car before walking down the steps. I stepped out and played footman, opening the rear door, and he got in, the glower still holding. The only thing I know of that Nero Wolfe dislikes more than riding in a car is riding in an airplane. He mistrusts all vehicles and endures them only when he feels he has absolutely no recourse.

Once settled—or as settled as Wolfe gets in a car—I eased from the curb, steering a course south and then east, eventually passing into Brooklyn through the tunnel at the Battery. The evening traffic was light, and I'm the best driver I know, but Wolfe sat rigid on the front half of the seat and clung to the strap as if it were a rip cord.

"We're about to cross the Verrazano-Narrows

Bridge," I said a few minutes later to be chatty, knowing he'd never laid eyes on this engineering wonder. "It is the longest single-span suspension bridge in the world, completed in 1964." He grunted his lack of enthusiasm at my knowledge of local trivia, so I clammed up for the rest of the drive.

It was early twilight when we pulled onto the blacktopped parking lot of the Silver Spire Tabernacle. About fifteen cars dozed under mercury-white lighting on the Vermont-sized expanse of tarmac, all of them near the entrance. I swung the Mercedes into the nearest available slot to the door. "This is the place," I said, shutting off the engine and turning to face Wolfe. "Chez Bay."

He scowled and I got out, opening the rear door on his side. As large as Wolfe is, he's never clumsy, and he climbed from the car as if he did it every day of his life, rather than on visits to the barber plus his annual trip to the Metropolitan Orchid Show. He stretched his legs and gave the building the once-over.

"Like I told you, it's a whopper," I said.

"That deceit should dwell in such a place."

"Shakespeare?"

"Paraphrased. I omitted the adjective 'gorgeous,' which this edifice clearly does not merit."

We went in through the glass double doors. A bony, dusty-haired guard in the seat occupied during the day by the redhead put down the dog-eared paperback western he was reading and squinted at us through half-glasses. "Sorry, church's closed now," the geezer droned after freeing a toothpick from his mouth. "First tour tomorrow's at nine."

"There's a meeting going on in the executive conference room," I told him evenly. "Reverend Bay is expecting us."

The guard peered doubtfully at a page in the loose-leaf notebook that lay open on his desk. "Don't have any record of visitors; what's the name?"

"Wolfe and Goodwin. Call Reverend Bay and tell him we're here," I snapped.

He shook his head. "Nope. Can't interrupt a meetin'."

I leaned so close to his leathery face that I could tell you what kind of spaghetti sauce he favored. "Look, I know damn well there's a phone in the conference room," I said, stressing each word. "Call Bay or I'll do it myself. And if I have to, you aren't going to like it."

The guard's watery eyes met mine, and he must have swallowed hard, because his Adam's apple bobbed. He picked up the instrument, punching a number.

"It's Perkins out front, sir," he rasped. "Sorry to disturb you, but there are two gentlemen here to see you. Named Wolfe and Goodwin . . . Yes, sir . . . Yes . . . All right, I'll tell them." He cradled the receiver, swallowed again, and glanced at me, then at Wolfe.

"The reverend'll be out in a minute," he wheezed, returning to his paperback and making a point of ignoring us. Wolfe looked at the angular contours of the guest chairs and grimaced, wisely choosing to stay on his feet. I did likewise. In about two minutes, a male silhouette appeared, moving toward us from the shadowy far end of the lobby, his footfalls echoing. Well before he emerged into the light, I knew it was Barnabas Bay.

"Mr. Wolfe. Mr. Goodwin. This is something of a surprise," Bay said, giving us a weak smile. "We're in the middle of our staff meeting, so—"

"Sir, I will be blunt," Wolfe told him. "Mr. Goodwin and I are cognizant of your meeting, and we chose this time to see you and your cadre together. The subject of our visit is Mr. Meade's death."

Bay, looking dapper in a brown herringbone sport coat, white shirt, and brown-and-gold-striped tie, puckered his lips and motioned us to move away from the guard's desk. When we were out of the old buzzard's earshot, Bay looked earnestly at Wolfe and cleared his throat.

"This is somewhat awkward, to say the least. As I have reiterated to both you and Mr. Goodwin, we all know that the killer—your Mr. Durkin—has long since been identified and charged. I know how much that must pain you, but I see no need for my staff to be put through any further pain by forcing them to relive the terrible tragedy. I feel I already indulged you by allowing Mr. Goodwin to question my people at length."

Wolfe, who hates conversing on his feet and who was angry to begin with, tapped his rubber-tipped walking stick once on the terrazzo, which for him is an act approaching violence. "Mr. Bay, either I talk to your assembled staff—I will not unduly prolong the session—or you will read what I have to say in tomorrow afternoon's edition of the *Gazette*. I assure you it will not be pleasurable reading."

I don't know what Bay was thinking, but it probably ran along the lines that he couldn't afford to take a chance on turning us away. "All right," he said after studying his tassel loafers. "I would first like to know what your message will be."

"No, sir, it doesn't work that way. You will all hear me simultaneously."

More silence. "This bothers me very much, I don't mind telling you, Mr. Wolfe. Can you give me *some* indication of what you're going to say?"

"I already have. It concerns Mr. Meade's murder. We are wasting both time and breath."

"All right." Bay sighed. "But I reserve the right as chair to cut off the discussion at any time."

Wolfe, knowing that once he got started nobody was going to cut him off, dipped his chin a fraction of an inch, and we followed Bay down a shadowy hallway.

The minister swung open the door to the conference room, and we were greeted by six shocked expressions. "We have guests," the minister announced before anyone could recover. "All of you have met Mr. Goodwin. And this is his employer, Mr. Nero Wolfe."

"What's all this about, Barney?" Sam Reese rose halfway out of his chair as the others nattered angrily. "These are the last people who ought to be showing their faces around here."

"Please, if I can explain," Bay said, holding up a hand. "I concede that this is unexpected, but Mr. Wolfe has asked for a few minutes to discuss . . . what happened to Roy."

"What's to discuss?" Marley Wilkenson barked.

"Durkin killed Roy—we all know it, and so do you, Barney."

"We went to Mr. Wolfe originally, seeking help," Bay said in a soothing but firm tone. "We owe him the courtesy of hearing what he has to say." That silenced them, at least for the moment, although nobody around the table looked to be oozing the milk of human kindness.

Bay gestured Wolfe to a chair at one end of the dark, highly polished conference table, and I helped him off with his overcoat. The chair was a couple of sizes smaller than he's used to, but he gamely wedged himself into it. I took a seat slightly behind and to the left of him. As Wolfe looked down the table, Lloyd Morgan was on his immediate right hand, with Sam Reese next to Morgan, then Carola, and finally Marley Wilkenson. Gillis was closest to Wolfe on the left, with Elise Bay and then her husband farther down that side. The table could seat at least twice the number that were gathered, so the far end was vacant.

Wolfe adjusted his bulk and studied the somber faces before him. "I can appreciate the genuine animosity with which you greet my presence," he said. "Each of you, save one, is convinced, with apparent good reason, that Mr. Durkin killed your colleague, and the evidence would seem to point in that direction."

"Amen," said Morgan, who got a glare from Bay.

Wolfe took a breath and went on. "You all embrace many tenets solely on faith, and for the moment, I ask you to accept something else on faith: My unswerving conviction that Fred Durkin is incapable of committing the crime with which he has been charged. Mr. Durkin is—"

"That's asking a lot of us," Carola Reese murmured, brushing a tendril of hair from her cheek.

"It is, madam, but I request your forbearance for only a short time. Mr. Durkin is, after all, innocent until proven guilty in our society."

"And you're going to tell us he's innocent because he was working for you, right?" Reese stuck out his chin belligerently.

Wolfe pursed his lips. "Sir, I intend to prove Mr. Durkin's innocence—by revealing the identity of the murderer. And to correct you, Mr. Durkin was *not* in my employ on this particular assignment. Now, does anyone—"

He was cut short by the ringing of the phone at Bay's elbow. "Yes. What? *Here?* Well . . . yes, bring them on back." Bay scowled and looked accusingly at Wolfe. "Two members of the police department have arrived. They apparently knew that you would be present tonight. You are straining the bounds of our hospitality." So now I knew how Wolfe had spent part of his time up in his room before we left. He'd called Cramer and didn't bother to tell me about it. This would be the subject of a future discussion between us.

"A murder has been committed," Wolfe responded to Bay, turning a palm up. "Although both you and I have vested interests in seeing this crime solved, the interests of the public, as represented by the police, supersede our own."

As if on cue, the door opened, and Inspector

Cramer and Sergeant Purley Stebbins pushed in, making the room seem suddenly smaller. "Inspector," Bay said, rising with an unsmiling nod, "I had not expected to see you tonight."

"I'm just as surprised as you are," Cramer gruffed. "But Sergeant Stebbins and I are here only as spectators."

"Isn't that more than a little bit unorthodox?" Roger Gillis asked in a high-pitched voice that barely missed being squeaky.

"Yes, but so's he." Cramer jabbed a thumb in Wolfe's direction. "He usually holds these charades at his place, and I've found over the years that it's a good idea to keep watch on them."

"So, in effect, Wolfe is calling the shots for the police department," Reese said, his chin still jutting out like a battering ram.

"He is *not!*" Cramer's face turned tomato-red, and a vein popped out in his neck. "He never has, and he never will, as long as I'm in this job."

"Inspector, our apologies; I know Sam meant no disrespect," Bay said, shifting to a soothing tone that awakened his southern drawl. "It's just that we are all on edge, as I'm sure you can understand. You are of course welcome here, as is the sergeant. Please take a seat."

Cramer and Stebbins settled in at the far end of the table, and all eyes switched from them to Wolfe as though they were following a tennis match.

He waited several seconds, for effect. "As I started to say earlier, does anyone quarrel with the statement that Mr. Meade was the least-liked member of this church's staff?"

That set them off again, like chained watchdogs baying at a burglar. When the noise died down, Elise Bay squared her shapely shoulders. "I think that's a very cheap thing to say, Mr. Wolfe," she responded quietly but firmly. Her husband reached over and patted her forearm as if to still her, but she pulled away, tossing him an irritated glance.

"I assure you it was not said in a spirit of either malice or caprice, madam. I simply stated what I know to be fact."

"How could you possibly begin to know anything about what goes on at the Silver Spire?" Morgan huffed. "You've never even been here before tonight. And until just now, you've never laid eyes on any of us, except for Barney."

"That is correct, but Mr. Goodwin functions competently as my eyes and ears. Through the years, I have found his observations to be keen and perceptive."

"Huh! So now we're being asked—or told—to validate the so-called findings of a private investigator," Morgan said.

"Now, now—we are caviling," Bay put in smoothly, laying a hand palm down on the tabletop. "Mr. Wolfe, I think it is fair to say that Roy Meade was somewhat abrasive at times in his pursuit of the Lord's work, but after all, so was St. Paul. Roy could be overly zealous, I know, but he also had a vision and a determination that made him truly a warrior for Christ, as I have said often—including to you. Every one of us around this table is the richer for having known him."

That was a spirited little speech, but I could tell

Wolfe wasn't bowled over by it. For that matter, it didn't exactly light up the faces of the Circle of Faith members, none of whom was about to spring up and applaud.

"I will stipulate that Mr. Meade was devoted in his faith and diligent in the fulfillment of his duties," Wolfe said dryly. "But was he popular with his co-workers? Hardly. Every member of this group had a reason to dislike him. The intensity of the animus varied, but it was palpable."

There was muttering, but no outright contradiction. "Is that an indirect way of suggesting that someone here—one of us—killed Roy?" Bay asked.

"Through the ages church leaders have been among those violating the laws Moses brought down from the mountain, including the sixth."

"What kind of answer is that?" Reese demanded.

"An honest one," Wolfe countered.

"Let's get on with it," Cramer snapped from the far end of the table. "Have you got something, or not?"

"I do, sir, and I do not feel you will deem your time wasted."

Gillis snorted. "Okay, since you're explaining everything, tell us who you think killed Roy."

"I prefer to first address the subject of the six Bible verses addressed to Mr. Bay, and why they were written. It was obvious to me that the missives were a subterfuge. Mr. Bay was never in any physical danger from the sender of those verses, but they served the purpose for which they were intended."

"Which was?" Morgan asked with a snort.

"To bring in an outside element, specifically a private investigator. Mr. Meade realized his adversary was up to something, and he took a defensive step, which I will detail later."

Elise Bay frowned. "What do you mean by adversary?"

Sighing, Wolfe made another futile attempt to get comfortable in his chair. "From the first, I was struck by this institution's handling of money," he said. "Thousands of dollars in currency are collected every week, and yet each of you has access to that money in its vault from about noon on Sunday until sometime Monday morning, when the counters arrive."

Bay jerked upright and set his jaw. "This is the Circle of Faith!" he said gravely, slapping a palm on the table and looking in turn at his colleagues. "I would trust each of them with my life, let alone the modest treasure we take in from our services."

"Money, particularly when readily and safely accessible, can be an overwhelming temptation," Wolfe responded. "Ecclesiastes said money answers all things. One among you was tempted, taking amounts not likely to be noticed, at least in the short run. This individual was found out by Royal Meade, however, and I can only surmise the circumstances of that discovery. Having caught the thief, Mr. Meade said nothing to anyone and arrogantly gave that individual a deadline in which to confess."

"If this is true—and I can't believe that it is—why wouldn't Roy have immediately told me about it?" Bay asked.

"Hubris. Mr. Meade thrived on the possession and exercise of power, as several of you here can testify. He wanted to control this unfortunate situation totally. However, he underestimated the resourcefulness and cunning of this adversary. He paid for that miscalculation with his life."

"Your 'adversary' business is hogwash!" Marley Wilkenson barked. "You haven't said one thing so far that points to anyone other than Durkin as the murderer."

"I shall rectify that oversight," Wolfe responded. "First, photocopies of the six threatening notes sent to Mr. Bay were found in a drawer of Mr. Meade's desk."

"You're making that up!" Reese charged, angrily jabbing a finger in Wolfe's direction.

"No, sir, I am not. Ask Mr. Cramer."

"Well?" Reese said, as he and everyone else at the table turned to face the inspector and Purley Stebbins.

"He's right," Cramer muttered.

"Inspector, why didn't you inform me of that discovery?" Bay asked evenly.

"I am not obligated to inform you—or anyone other than my superiors—of developments in the course of a homicide investigation," Cramer growled.

"But Wolfe knows about them!" Morgan spat.

"I have been known to share information with him on occasion," Cramer shot back. "I see no reason to justify that to you."

Morgan bristled. "That's a pretty arrogant attitude for a public servant to take with—"

"Now, now, please," Bay said smoothly. "We are not here to fight with one another. I would like to ask one of you—Mr. Cramer, Mr. Wolfe, whoever cares to answer—what you think about those copies being in Roy's desk."

"One of my men found them. But ask Wolfe, it's his show," Cramer grumped, folding his arms across his chest.

Wolfe inhaled deeply, wishing he had beer. "Mr. Meade did not place those threatening Bible verses in the offering pouches. If he had, he surely would not have kept self-implicating copies. Those, of course, were planted in his desk drawer by the individual who stole the money from the vault, who created the original notes—and who later shot Mr. Meade."

"Oh, come on," Wilkenson groaned. "This gets sillier by the minute. If one adopts your theory, wacky as it is, then what was to be gained by putting the photocopies in Roy's desk?"

"A valid question. The author of those notes wanted them to be found and tied to Mr. Meade."

"Why?" Wilkenson asked.

"To discredit Mr. Meade before he was able to publicly accuse the thief. From the first, Mr. Meade knew who was writing the notes, although he probably was unaware that a duplicate set had been slipped into one of his own desk drawers. However, as self-confident as he was, he sensed he might be in some physical danger and countered one series of biblical passages with another. He realized that if anything were to happen to incapacitate him, others on the staff—including the thief—would surely go through his papers. He needed to veil his message, and then hope someone deciphered it. For a minister, what better way than in a listing of seemingly innocuous Bible verses? With Mr. Bay's approval, Mr. Goodwin searched the dead man's office. I had instructed him to be alert for biblical notations, and he discovered a sheet of paper listing seven verses, in what a member of the church staff confirmed was Mr. Meade's handwriting. I read these verses in each of the Bibles in my library, seeking a pattern.

"I found none, but I was making an easy job difficult. Genius frequently overlooks the obvious," Wolfe observed immodestly. "Far later than I should have, I finally comprehended Mr. Meade's message. Mr. Goodwin will now pass out copies of the verses, as taken from the New International Version of the Bible. Upon reading them, some of you may well wonder where my brain was as I read the passages."

I pulled the sheets from the envelope and walked around the table, placing one in front of each of them, including Cramer and Stebbins. For close to a minute, everyone read before Bay broke the silence.

"I find nothing specific here," he said, shrugging and looking at the others around the table. "Unless I'm in a total fog, there seems to be no common thread linking these texts."

"Anyone else?" Wolfe said, raising his eyebrows. "No? Perhaps you all are making the same mistake I did. I doggedly persisted in seeking a substantive message in the passages." I smiled inwardly; never have I heard a relapse described as such hard work.

"Okay, you've stumped us," Gillis snapped, slapping the sheet. "That is, if there's really any point at all to this."

Wolfe dipped his head a fraction of an inch. "I sympathize with your frustration. After realizing that there was no textual link among these seven, I sought a cipher. When I found it, I chastised myself at its childlike simplicity. Mr. Meade drew up this list of verses with the expectation that it would be found only if some grave misfortune befell him, which would make it in effect his last word. There are seven verses in all. The first, from I Timothy, serves only to establish the subject: the love of money as a force for evil. Now study the other six, in the order Mr. Meade set them down, and take the first letter in the last word of each."

Elise Bay spoke first. "It spells . . . Morgan," she said tensely, as Purley Stebbins got up and moved silently around the table, stopping behind an ashen-faced Lloyd Morgan.

"This is ridiculous and farfetched," Morgan cried. "I'm not going to sit here and—" He started to rise, and Purley Stebbins gently but firmly pushed him back down with a beefy hand on his shoulder.

"Mr. Wolfe, an explanation is in order," Bay said, his composure ruffled.

"Mr. Morgan had been taking money from the Sunday collections. How much and for how long— you'll have to ask him. Mr. Meade found out about this thievery—very likely catching him in the act. That's not surprising, given that he, Meade, spent so much time in the building. He gave Mr. Morgan a deadline to confess his embezzlement, perhaps giving him the opportunity to repay the money."

"Barney, this is absurd. Those letters spelling my name, that's just a silly coincidence," Morgan said loudly. Beads of perspiration began to form on his face.

"Coincidence? Hardly," Wolfe replied. "Depending on the frequency with which letters occur in a language, the odds of six letters from an alphabet of twenty-six coming up randomly in a specific order is something over one hundred million to one." He turned toward Bay. "Shortly after Mr. Morgan was discovered pilfering funds, he began writing the ominous notes, which were, as I said earlier, a subterfuge to bring a private investigator to the scene. He had been given a grace period by Mr. Meade—a fatal mistake, as it turned out. He persuaded you that a detective was needed to find the writer. I was the first choice, and I declined. Mr. Goodwin then recommended Fred Durkin.

"Mr. Morgan's hope was that the investigator would search desks and discover the photocopies of the notes, thereby placing Mr. Meade in an untenable position. His logic was that once Mr. Meade had been accused of writing those notes, any countercharge he made would seem the attempt of a man desperately trying to shift the spotlight of accusation from himself. It had not been Mr. Morgan's original intention to kill Royal Meade, only to discredit him.

"He encouraged Mr. Durkin to spend as much time as he needed—at any time of day—in this building. His plan foundered, however, because Fred Durkin is not by nature a desk-rifler. Mr. Morgan, who could not very well suggest that Fred prowl through desks, grew frustrated and desperate, and on the night of the fateful session in this room, he suddenly saw an opportunity to forever silence his antagonist. When Fred lost his temper and Mr. Bay called for a recess to allow tempers to cool, his plan coalesced. He knew Fred wore a shoulder holster and that he took it off along with his suitcoat while in the building.

And he also knew where he hung the holster and pistol."

"So did everybody here," Morgan said in a frantic tone. "You're singling me out to try to save your pal."

Wolfe ignored him. "Mr. Morgan knew he had fifteen minutes, and he also knew, as did everyone else employed by the church, that both the doors and the walls are so thick as to be virtually soundproof. He went to his office to meditate, but stayed only a short time, probably no more than a minute. He reentered the hall, making sure it was deserted, and got Mr. Durkin's pistol from its holster. He then went to Mr. Meade's office, entering it, probably without knocking, and closing the door behind him. Royal Meade undoubtedly looked up, surprised to see his colleague during a time decreed for solitary contemplation. At close range, five feet or less, he was an easy target quickly dispatched, even by someone not familiar with handguns. Mr. Morgan probably had a handkerchief between his hand and the handle of the gun to prevent fingerprints.

"In one decisive move, he apparently eliminated his problem. He had committed murder, and to compound the iniquity, he was perfectly content to let another individual suffer for it." The last sentence was uttered with more contempt than I have ever heard in Wolfe's voice.

Bay turned to Morgan. "Do you have anything you'd like to say, Lloyd?" he asked hoarsely. Morgan opened his mouth, but no sound came. He shook his head and looked at the tabletop.

"Let us bow in prayer," Bay said. "Dear Lord, we

thank you for your presence with us, and we ask your guidance. This is a troubling time for your church in this place, and we seek your help. . . ." He stopped because of the racking sobs that came from Morgan, who had buried his face in his hands and was shaking. ". . . We know that in this fallen world we all are sinners, and that no one among us is fit to judge any other. Only you can judge, and it is in you that we put our faith, our trust, and our unending love. Please be with us now and forever, we pray, in the name of your son Jesus Christ. Amen."

Four of us—Wolfe, Cramer, Stebbins, and I—had not bowed, but were watching the others, all of whom did pray. Morgan was still sobbing as Stebbins helped him to his feet and, after a nod from Cramer, began to recite the Miranda warning: "You have the right to remain silent . . ." I didn't hear the rest, because I was on my way out the door, going to the nearest office to call Fred Durkin.

EIGHTEEN

From the telephone in Gillis's office, I reached Fred at home, giving him the happy news that he would not be boarding with the state after all. I then called Lon Cohen, who was still at the paper, and fed him the highlights of the evening. As usual, he wanted more, and I suggested he call both Cramer and Bay. "I can't stay on the line with you forever," I told him. "My boss has seen all he wants to of Staten Island. And he doesn't like riding in a car after dark even more than he doesn't like riding in a car in daylight."

"What I don't get, Archie, is why Wolfe left the comfort of his abode to wrap this one up," Lon said.

"Okay, here's my reading, not for publication. One, he was so damned angry that a would-be client had the gall to try to hire him to use him—and me—in a setup. And two, the jerk had connived so that Durkin would take the fall. Now, there's been lots of times when Wolfe can take Fred or leave him, but he *is* family, and to Nero Wolfe, that means plenty. Also, it's just barely possible that he didn't think I could get on the horn and cajole the whole bunch of them to come to the brownstone."

The next morning, following a grade-A breakfast, I was in the office reading the *Times*, which had no mention of the night's activities at the Silver Spire, meaning Lon and the *Gazette* had themselves a scoop for their early-afternoon editions. The phone rang, and I recognized the voice on the other end. It was Barnabas Bay, who wanted to pay us a visit that morning. I told him Wolfe wouldn't be down from the plant rooms until eleven, and the reverend responded that he'd be there at ten past the hour.

When Wolfe descended at eleven sharp, I didn't mention the call or the impending visit, figuring the surprise would enliven his day. Sure enough, the doorbell rang at exactly eleven-ten. "A well-known preacher is standing out on the stoop," I told Wolfe after I'd walked down the hall and peered at Bay through the one-way glass. "Do I let him in?"

"Confound it, yes," he said, making a face.

The Barnabas Bay I admitted into the brownstone had aged years in the last few hours. Looking all of forty-eight, he nodded a grim-faced greeting and made his second trip down the hall to the office.

"Good day, sir," Wolfe said as the minister dropped into the red leather chair. "Would you like coffee?"

"No, thank you," Bay answered listlessly, as hoarse as he had been last night. "I can't stay long. I am here for two reasons, really. The first is to apologize for refusing to believe you when you insisted that Mr. Durkin was innocent."

Wolfe raised his shoulders a fraction of an inch and let them drop. "No one wants to believe that one's colleague is a criminal," he said. "I should think that would be particularly true in a religious institution."

"It is. After you left last night, Lloyd told the police and me that he'd taken just a few dollars from the offering the first time, for, of all things, two dress shirts. You know, he never complained to me about his salary not being enough," the minister said in an agonized tone. "Anyway, he promised himself that he would return the money a week or two later, but he never did. Instead, he took more—the next time to help cover expenses for a vacation he and his wife were taking. He thinks he dipped in about six or seven times over several months. He told us—between sobs—that it got easier each time. And then, one Sunday night late, Roy caught him in the vault, and, well . . ." Bay slumped in the chair and shook his head.

"The character flaw was always there," Wolfe said. "Eventually it would have manifested itself in some way, regardless of his salary."

"Perhaps. But, obviously, something essential is lacking in my leadership. I spent most of the night praying, and I haven't got any answers yet as to what God has in mind for me now. But I didn't come here to talk about myself. The second reason for my visit, Mr. Wolfe, is that despite the trauma we're going through, the Silver Spire owes you a debt, one that I want to pay. I know your charges are high, but on behalf of the church, I am prepared to negotiate a fee, and I will not be a hard bargainer."

"There has been no agreement between us, sir.

You are under no obligation whatever," Wolfe said, turning a hand over.

"But I am, and it's the most binding obligation of all: that of a Christian to do the right thing."

Wolfe remained still and silent for several seconds and then came forward in his chair. "I have relatives in Europe to whom I send money each month. I will give you their addresses, and if you so choose, you can send a modest contribution to them. Their lives are far from easy."

Bay liked that idea and took the names of Wolfe's cousins. We later learned that each of them was receiving a monthly money order from the Silver Spire.

"Actually, I do have another question," Bay said sheepishly. "It falls under the category of curiosity—nothing more." Wolfe signaled him to continue with a nod.

Bay nodded back. "You may only be able to guess at this, but why didn't Roy at least tell his wife, Sara, about having caught Lloyd?"

Wolfe shifted in his chair. "As I stated last night, hubris. Mr. Meade was self-confident to the point of arrogance and preferred to act completely alone. He felt that the more he shared his knowledge, the more his role as authority figure—and in this case, enforcer—would be diminished. He was not unlike Shakespeare's Henry the Fifth, who on the eve of the Battle at Agincourt proclaimed, 'The fewer men, the greater share of honor.' "

Bay sighed. "Maybe you're right. Lloyd also told us last night that Roy gave him a deadline so that he could repay the money, as you had suggested. But Lloyd also felt very strongly that Roy was enjoying his discomfort as the days passed. I hate to believe that."

"But you do believe it."

"Yes, I do. I have always been aware of Roy's flaws, whether I wanted to admit it or not. But we all have them. I've never been more aware of my own than at this moment," Bay said as he got to his feet, which seemed to be an effort. "Thank you, Mr. Wolfe."

Wolfe nodded as I followed the minister down the hall and let him out, watching as he got into the back seat of the blue sedan at the curb.

NINETEEN

About six months after the trial in which Lloyd Morgan received a life sentence, Barnabas Bay stepped down as head of the Tabernacle of the Silver Spire. The *Gazette* story on his resignation of course had a rehash of Meade's murder and Morgan's conviction, but the paper's religion editor apparently could not get Bay to make any connection between that and what was termed his "unexpected departure." The minister's only quote in the story was: "This is a time of spiritual renewal and rededication for me and for my family. We leave with the comforting knowledge that the Spire ministry is in able hands." The *Times* story carried exactly the same quote and nothing more from him. The last I heard, Bay was somewhere in Florida writing another book on his religious beliefs and philosophy.

Both stories also said that a thirty-five-year-old minister named Foster from California was the new head man at the Silver Spire, and that Gillis, Wilkenson, and Reese had been asked to remain on the staff. The *Gazette*'s religion editor, while questioning Foster's experience as an administrator, described him as "stirring and dynamic in the pulpit, biblically knowledgeable and a true spellbinder who will be a worthy preaching successor to Barnabas Bay, both at the big church itself and in its powerful and far-reaching television ministry."

I'll take his word for it.

ABOUT THE AUTHOR

ROBERT GOLDSBOROUGH, award-winning author of *Murder in E Minor, Death on Deadline, The Bloodied Ivy, The Last Coincidence,* and *Fade to Black,* is a longtime Nero Wolfe fan and expert. He is the recipient of the eighth annual Nero Award, given by the Wolfe Pack. Formerly an editor with the *Chicago Tribune,* he is now an editor with *Advertising Age* and *Business Marketing.* He lives in Wheaton, Illinois, where he is at work on his next Nero Wolfe mystery, *The Missing Chapter.*

If you enjoyed Robert Goldsborough's SILVER
SPIRE, you will applaude the next appearance of
Nero Wolfe in

THE MISSING CHAPTER
By Robert Goldsborough.

Available in hardcover from your bookseller in
December 1993.

Y ou're almost fifteen minutes early," I told the elegant-looking visitor who stood erect on our front stoop. "We don't deny admission on a technicality like that, though. And I've seen your picture in the newspapers—more than once. Come on in."

"Thank you," Horace Vinson said with a smile, smoothing well-tended salt-and-pepper hair that had been ruffled by rude April winds. "I thought the cab ride down here would take a lot longer. You, of course, are Archie Goodwin. I, too, have seen your picture in the papers. And I recognize your voice from yesterday."

I grinned back and held out a paw. "Guilty as charged. He won't be down until eleven, but there's no reason you can't park yourself in his office. I'll even keep you company at no extra charge," I said as I hung his expensive Burberry on a peg and led him down the hall.

Vinson squinted cornflower-blue eyes as he stood in the doorway to the largest room in the house and nodded approvingly. "Just as I pictured it. Arguably the most famous work space in Manhattan. And from a quick look, very possibly the most comfortable, too."

"Unless you are a murderer Nero Wolfe is about to finger. Have a seat. Can I get you coffee?"

Vinson said yes, heavy on the cream, as he settled into the red leather chair in front of the desk. I went to the kitchen, where Fritz Brenner, chef *extraordinaire*, keeps a pot warm all morning. Fritz looked at me anxiously as I filled a cup with java and the cow's finest. "Too early to tell," I responded to his unspoken question. "Of course Mr. Wolfe hasn't even seen him yet, let alone heard him out. If something of interest develops, you'll be the fourth to know."

Fritz sighed and turned back to building the cassoulet Castelnaudary that Wolfe and I would be devouring in the dining room in a little more than two hours. He frets when Wolfe isn't working, which means he almost always frets. Fritz figures we're constantly on the brink of bankruptcy, and nothing I ever tell him to the contrary seems to help.

Actually, this time I was more than a little worried myself. We hadn't done any work in months, unless you count the child's play in which we—make that I—collared the Fifth Avenue jewelry store clerk who made a cute little game of substituting passable imitations for the expensive ice in his employer's display cases and carting the genuine articles away. It took all of three days before I doped out which of eight employees in the pricey store was making the switches. I caught the poor wretch in the act, and our reward was enough to keep Wolfe in beer, books, and bouillabaisse for a couple of moons.

Not that we hadn't had other recent opportunities for gainful employment, as in a pair of potential cases, each of which would have given the bank balance a healthy transfusion. But both times, Wolfe found excuses for taking a pass. The real reason he turned thumbs down—and I told him so—was downright laziness, combined with a contrary streak as wide as his back.

I should correct myself. *Lazy* is not a word to be strictly applied to Nero Wolfe. Stubborn, yes, but not lazy. He allots four hours every day—nine to eleven in the morning and four to six in the afternoon—to nurturing the ten thousand orchids in the plant rooms on the roof of the brownstone. Most of the rest of his waking hours are spent either in the dining room devouring Fritz's superb lunches and dinners, or in his office, where he devours anywhere from five to ten books a week, sometimes juggling three at a time. Okay, the guy's not doing push-ups, but his mind is in high gear, so scratch the lazy comment.

My roles in the operation are varied. I handle Wolfe's correspondence, balance the books, work with our live-in orchid nurse, Theodore Horstmann, to keep the germination records up to date, and serve as so-called man of action when the two of us are working at being private detectives—duly licensed by the Sovereign State of New York. I also function as a burr under Wolfe's saddle when he doesn't feel like working. Obviously, I hadn't been a real good burr of late, and I'd been indulging in mopery on that April Tuesday morning when the phone rang.

"Nero Wolfe's office, Archie Goodwin speaking."

"Mr. Goodwin, my name is Horace Vinson. I am in the publishing business, and I would like to engage Nero Wolfe to investigate a murder."

The good old direct approach; that's a guaranteed way to get my attention. Another is name recognition, and I immediately recognized Vinson's name. "Who got murdered?" I asked, poising a pencil above my stenographer's pad.

"Charles Childress. He was shot a week ago."

"The writer," I said. "Found in his apartment in Greenwich Village last Tuesday, an apparent suicide. Three paragraphs in the *Gazette* the next day, somewhere back around page thirteen."

The response was a snort. "Suicide, hell! Charles was killed. Those idiots who masquerade as police in this town don't think so, but I know so. Are you interested or not?"

I told Horace Vinson I'd take it up with Wolfe, which I did when he descended from the plant rooms. That brought the glare I was expecting, so I got up and walked all of three paces from my desk to his, placing a computer printout on his blotter. "That," I told Wolfe, "is the result of your consistent refusal to reenter the work force. You may recognize those figures as our bank balance. Note how the last nine entries have been withdrawals. Note also that if we continue at the current pace, we will be forced to file for bankruptcy after another fourteen withdrawals."

"Your mathematics are suspect, as usual," Wolfe said with an air of unconcern.

"Okay, maybe you've got some other funds tucked away, a fortune you've never told me about. Even so, given our monthly expenses, you'd need at least—"

"Archie, shut up!"

"Yes, sir."

Wolfe closed his eyes, presumably because looking at me was more than he could bear. He stayed that way for over a minute, then awoke and favored me with another glare. "Confound it, call Mr. Vinson, tell him to be here tomorrow at eleven."

Which is why I was sitting in the office chatting with Horace Vinson, editor-in-chief of Monarch Press, at eleven the next morning when the groan of the elevator announced Wolfe's descent from the plant rooms. The lord of the manor paused at the office door, dipped his head a fraction of an inch in our guest's direction, then detoured around his desk, placing a raceme of orchids in a vase on the blotter before settling into the chair that was expressly constructed to support his seventh of a ton. "Mr. Vinson," he said. His version of an effusive greeting.

"Mr. Wolfe, good to meet you. My God, those flowers are stunning."

"*Doritaenopsis,* a crossing of *Phalaenopsis* and *Doritis,*" Wolfe replied. Vinson may not have known it, but he had said precisely the right thing; Nero Wolfe loves to have his orchids gushed over.

"Would you like more coffee or something else to drink?" he asked Vinson. "I am going to have beer."

"Not just yet. Mr. Goodwin told you why I am here?"

"The death of a writer. Mr. Childress. One of your authors, I believe."

Vinson shifted in the red leather chair and studied his pearl cufflink. "Yes, one of my authors," he said huskily. "He was shot last week—eight days ago now—in his apartment in the Village."

Wolfe paused to pour beer from one of two chilled bottles Fritz had just brought in. "I read the newspaper accounts." He frowned at the foam in his glass. "The police have labeled it a suicide."

"Nonsense! Charles had everything to live for. He was a relatively successful writer, he had a terrific future, and he was about to be married to a beautiful woman whom he loved and doted on."

"He was shot with his own gun, and when Mr. Goodwin telephoned the police yesterday at my direction, he was informed by Sergeant Stebbins of Homicide that the only fingerprints on the weapon were his own," Wolfe said evenly.

Vinson leaned forward and placed his palms on his knees. "Mr. Wolfe, surely you have seen enough murders to realize that killers know how to make their handiwork seem like something else."

"I have," Wolfe said, drinking beer and dabbing his lips with a handkerchief. "Tell me why someone would want to kill Mr. Childress."

Vinson's well-tailored shoulders sagged, and he dropped back into the chair with a sigh. "All right. First off, Charles was, well, not the most pleasant person you'd ever be likely to run into. Some people found him boastful and arrogant, to say the least."

"Do you agree with that assessment?"

"Mr. Wolfe, Charles Childress was a talented writer—not brilliant, but with an ability that I felt was soon to come to full flower, if you'll pardon the hyperbole. And he possessed a well-developed sense of self. He knew what his strengths were. And he wasn't the least bit reticent about proclaiming them."

"Fanfaronade is not a trait conducive to the development of friendships, but rarely is it the primary stimulus for murder," Wolfe observed. Yep, I was there. He really said it.

"Fanfaronade, as you term it, was only a part of Charles's problem," Vinson replied without missing a beat, forming a chapel with his long, bony fingers. "He also was contentious, combative, and exceedingly vengeful. Does the name Wilbur Hobbs mean anything to you?"

Wolfe grunted. "He attempts to review books for the *Gazette*."

That brought a slight smile to the editor's angular face. "Well said. As you probably know, Charles was the continuator of the long and extremely popular series of detective novels, the Sergeant Barnstable stories, which were originated by Darius Sawyer in the forties."

"I learned as much from the newspaper reports on Mr. Childress's death," Wolfe replied dryly. "My current schedule does not allow for the reading of detective fiction, let alone its so-called continuation by a second author."

Vinson shrugged and let his eyes travel over Wolfe's bookshelves. "Actually, some detective stories qualify as solid literature, better certainly than a lot of the nongenre work being turned out today. And I happen to think Charles did a fine job of capturing the spirit and flavor of Sawyer's writing. Of course, my opinion could be termed suspect, as I am the one who picked Charles to be the series continuator after Sawyer died. I had read the books he'd done previously, for another publisher, and I felt he had potential to ultimately go beyond writing mysteries. Anyway, Wilbur Hobbs has been rough on all three of Charles's Barnstable books, and he was particularly savage in reviewing the last one, which we published about six weeks ago."

Wolfe drained his glass. He refilled it from the second bottle. I read the review. How have other critics treated Mr. Childress's work?"

"Mixed," Vinson said. "Most range from mildly favorable to mildly negative, but nothing like Hobbs, who is a nasty, vituperative little man. As you know, his *Gazette* review of the most recent Barnstable book, *Death in the North Meadow,* was incredibly mean-spirited. Among other things, he called it a 'towering exercise in mimicry' and said that 'Any self-respecting lover of mysteries should treat this volume as if it were a radioactive cobalt isotope.' "

Vinson exhaled. "Charles never took criticism particularly well, and Hobbs's piece—it occupied all of page three in the *Gazette*'s Sunday book review section—really lit his wick. He fired off an article to the *Manhattan Literary Times* blasting Hobbs. I tried to talk him out of submitting the piece—there's almost never anything to be gained by lashing back at a critic—but he was adamant. Are you familiar with the *MLT*?"

Wolfe said no, and Vinson went on. "It's a self-styled avant-garde weekly tabloid that thrives on controversy. Of course they printed Charles's article, in which he attacked Hobbs as 'a preening poseur, a peacock, a dandified and self-important satrap who is trying desperately, yea, pitifully, to become an arbiter of public taste, which is roughly equivalent to John Travolta trying to fit into Astaire's white tie and tails.' Quite a sentence, eh? But that wasn't the worst of it. Charles all but accused Hobbs of being on the take, of accepting gifts—financial and otherwise—from authors and publishers whose works he praises in print."

"Is there substance to that charge?"

Vinson set his jaw, then nodded reluctantly. "Possibly. It has been rumored in the publishing community for years, but nobody had ever come out and said anything publicly before. There's no question about Hobbs having his favorites—both among writers and publishing houses. You can pretty well predict how he's going to react to a book—with fawning praise or fiery vitriol—depending on who the writer and publisher are. Hobbs doesn't like Monarch, never has, despite our having had two Pulitzer Prize winners and five National Book Awards in the last years. Why doesn't he like us?" Vinson asked, anticipating Wolfe's question. "Because nobody in our house, from me on down to the lowest editorial assistant, will kowtow to the little viper. We've never made any secret of our feelings about the man, and I've even written to the publisher of the *Gazette* complaining about the obvious bias in Hobbs's reviews. And he certainly didn't like Charles Childress. After the *MLT* piece came out, almost a month ago, Hobbs phoned me in a fury. He made loud noises about a lawsuit, but that's the last I heard about it."

Wolfe leaned back and scowled. "Has Mr. Hobbs ever approached anyone at your company soliciting money or other favors?"

"A few years ago, several editors on our staff mentioned he tossed out some veiled hints to them that he was open to 'offers,' is how I think he termed it," Vinson responded sourly. "Both editors assured me they pretended they didn't understand what he was talking about. Apparently, Hobbs did not press the issue with either of them, but soon after those episodes, we started getting execrable reviews from him on virtually every one of our books."

"Is it commonplace for book reviewers to accept *cadeaux* from publishers?"

"It is *not*. God knows I've been angry at reviewers through the years, but always because I disagreed with their literary opinions. Then Wilbur Hobbs came along. With him, I question the motives *for* those opinions."

"And you suggest that Mr. Hobbs committed murder in retaliation for the scathing indictment Mr. Childress had penned about him?"

"I see that as a distinct possibility," Vinson responded with a scowl of his own. "Although it is by no means the only possibility."

"Indeed?" Wolfe raised his eyebrows.

Vinson nodded grimly. "I can think of two other people who might also take satisfaction in helping to end Charles Childress's life."

Wolfe's eyebrows stayed up. "Sir, I confess amazement that book publishing holds such potential for violence."

"I wish I could honestly tell you I was amazed myself," Vinson replied earnestly. "But I've been in this business for forty years, and there's damn little that can surprise me anymore."

I could tell that Wolfe was still amazed, but he pulled himself together long enough to finish the beer in his glass.